ASK YOU LATER

BOOKS BY JAN THOMPSON

CITY/COASTAL/BEACH ROMANCE

Seaside Chapel (7 Books)

JanThompson.com/seaside

Savannah Sweethearts (12 Books)

JanThompson.com/savannah

Vacation Sweethearts (8 Books)

JanThompson.com/vacation

ROMANTIC SUSPENSE/THRILLERS

Protector Sweethearts (6 Books)

JanThompson.com/protector

Defender Sweethearts (6 Books)

JanThompson.com/defender

Binary Hackers (4 Books)

JanThompson.com/binary

JanThompson.com/books

ASK YOU LATER

SAVANNAH SWEETHEARTS
BOOK ONE

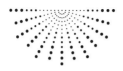

JAN THOMPSON

GEORGIA
PRESS

ASK YOU LATER (SAVANNAH
SWEETHEARTS BOOK 1)

Copyright © 2017 Jan Edttii Lim Thompson

Book News: JanThompson.com/newsletter
Author Website: JanThompson.com
Published by Georgia Press LLC

This novel is a work of fiction. Any resemblance to actual
persons, places, events, things, and ideas are all products of the
author's active imagination.

Scripture taken from the New King James Version®. Copyright
© 1982 by Thomas Nelson. Used by permission. All rights
reserved.

eBook Cover Design: Georgia Press LLC
Paperback Cover Design: Georgia Press and Deranged Doctor
Design

eBook ISBN 978-1-944188-34-4
Paperback ISBN 978-1-944188-35-1

To my Lord and Savior, Jesus Christ, who died on the cross to save me from my sins and rose again from the grave to give me eternal life in heaven.

For God so loved the world that He gave His only begotten Son, that whoever believes in Him should not perish but have everlasting life.
—John 3:16

READ A FREE EBOOK IN THE SAME STORY WORLD

Set in Georgia, South Carolina, and Tennessee, this clean and wholesome Christian romance tells the story of art gallery archivist Sheryl Breckenridge and world-famous sculptor Winton Pace. Read this ebook for free!

Time for Me (A Vacation Sweethearts Prequel)
JanThompson.com/time-free

ABOUT THE SAVANNAH SWEETHEARTS SERIES

Welcome to the new south! From *USA Today* bestselling author Jan Thompson come these clean and wholesome, sweet and inspirational Christian romances set in the coastal city of Savannah, Georgia, and on the beaches of Tybee Island by the Atlantic Ocean.

Meet a group of multiracial and multiethnic churchgoing Christians who love the Lord, work hard in their careers, and seek God's will for their love lives. Against a backdrop of ocean, sand, and sun, these inspirational romances showcase aspects of the human need for God and for one another.

Have some tea, settle in a comfortable reading chair, and enjoy these sweet celebrations of faith, hope, and love in Jesus Christ.

SAVANNAH SWEETHEARTS

- Book 1: Ask You Later
- Book 2: Know You More
- Book 3: Tell You Soon
- Book 4: Draw You Near
- Book 5: Cherish You So
- Book 6: Walk You There
- Book 7: Love You Always
- Book 8: Kiss You Now
- Book 9: Find You Again
- Book 10: Wish You Joy
- Book 11: Call You Home
- Book 12: Let You Go

While Savannah Sweethearts books can be read as standalone stories, you can see a bigger picture of the Riverside Chapel community and get a glimpse of the futures of previous characters if you read Books 1-12 in order.

YOU ARE READING ASK YOU LATER

SAVANNAH SWEETHEARTS BOOK 1

He lives and breathes expressive art.
She has no time for his type of fluff.

A struggling artist tries to get his recycled mix media creations displayed at a local art gallery now run by the owner's daughter who has zero appreciation for his folk art.

SOPHIE'S SELECTIONS...

A freelance technical writer who writes obscure user guides that nobody reads and engineering manuals for little-use heavy machinery, Sophie Kowalski's career is filled with black ink on white paper, legalese and technical stuff that few people care about—except for proofreaders and publishers.

When her dad has a nasty fall outside his art gallery and breaks his leg in several places, Sophie is forced to run Simon's Gallery for a couple of months while her dad recovers from his unfortunate accident.

Immediately, Sophie removes what she considers "junk art" in the gallery, and cancels several exhibitions by lesser-known artists, replacing them with more famous works that showcase clean lines and minimalism...

LEON'S LEGACY...

A poor and struggling mix-media local artist, Leonardo "Leon" Watts thinks he has finally turned a corner in his career when Simon Kowalski of the reputable Simon's Gallery on River Street decides to display his recycled sculptures that showcase everyday life.

That is, before Simon tumbles on the cobblestones, ends up in the hospital, and takes two months off to recover. Standing in Leon's way is Simon's daughter, Sophie, now running the gallery however she wants and in whichever way she pleases.

She says that Leon's displays are "garbage" and shouldn't see the light of day. Well, technically, he only uses discarded materials he finds in junkyards and recycling centers...

Still, who is she to judge his art?

When Leon decides to educate that unimaginative Sophie on the value of his brand of everyman artwork, he gets more than he is prepared to handle, as his heart begins to express itself in unexpected ways...

Formerly the prequel, *Ask You Later* is the new Book 1 in *USA Today* bestselling author Jan Thompson's Savannah Sweethearts, a Christian romance collection set in the coastal city of Savannah, Georgia, and on the nearby beaches of Tybee Island by the Atlantic Ocean.

Ask You Later (Savannah Sweethearts Book 1):
JanThompson.com/ask

Savannah Sweethearts:
JanThompson.com/sweethearts

For book news, sign up for Jan's mailing list:
JanThompson.com/newsletter

ASK YOU LATER

CHAPTER ONE

*N*o *way.*

Sophie Kowalski stared at the pile of laundry in front of her, right in the middle of the polished oak art gallery floor. The brightly painted-over stack of old clothes glued together and standing seven feet tall had a funny smell coming out of it. Sophie wasn't sure if that was the fresh glue and paint.

It was something else.

A stink.

Her eyes watered.

"There's just no way." She didn't know how else to say it to the gallery manager, standing next to her, clutching his iPhone like it were a lifeline out of here.

"Your dad..." Baxter began to say. His voice

trailed off, as if anything more would take away from the impact of his words.

Your. Dad.

Sophie didn't back down. "There's just no way this pile of junk would be featured in this gallery while I'm here."

As if Baxter hadn't heard her, Sophie repeated herself a third time. "No way."

Baxter cleared his throat.

Funny how it went. They all cleared their throats whenever Sophie put a foot down. Her editors. Her multiple publishers. Her publicists. Everyone.

But she knew she was right.

"Your dad said—uh..." Baxter didn't finish his sentence.

Do you want to be fired?

"Dad is at home resting from his broken leg. I'm in charge of this gallery until he comes back to work. But you knew that."

Sophie had kept her voice even and low, but she knew the other employees had heard her. That was the point. The fact that she was the temporary director of Simon's Gallery had to be established before order could be put into place. They all had to know that Dad had given her the authority over this gallery for the next couple of months.

"As long as I'm running this place, the last thing

we want is to be in the red," Sophie continued. "That would mean cutbacks and layoffs. We don't want that, do we?"

"No, no. We don't want that. No, ma'am."

"Good. I say no to this piece of garbage."

"Yes, ma'am."

"My dad has worked so hard to build this gallery. Let's not ruin it."

Baxter nodded. "W-what about the other local artists' displays?"

"They can stay."

"He might say you're singling him out."

"He who?"

"The sculptor. He delivered everything himself."

"Then he can take it right back." *What is his problem?* "I want this out of here before we open at ten."

Baxter stared at his iPhone. "That's in fifteen minutes."

"Shouldn't be too hard to haul this away in five minutes. I want the floor cleaned afterwards."

"What do I tell him?"

Sophie started walking to the next display. "We don't have to display every art piece."

"Your dad signed the consignment contract. I witnessed it."

"I read it. It says Simon's Gallery can terminate

3

the contract at any time. In this case, I make the call since I'm standing in for Dad. I don't want any of this man's artwork, sculpture, mixed media, or whatnot displayed anywhere in this building."

"He'll want to be compensated."

"Whatever's spelled out in the contract." Sophie froze in front of a pile of rusty forks and spoons and burnt pots and pans. "What in the world is this mess?"

"Ah..." Baxter was right next to her in a jiffy. "That's his work too."

Sophie rolled her eyes. "What is this? Junk Day?"

"*Recycle Day*. This week's theme from his *Home Life* series."

She glanced at her watch. "Ten minutes. You have ten minutes."

"He'll want an explanation. We told him every-thing was fine."

"Have him call me."

The gallery manager's eyes darted toward the back hallway of the gallery. Voices echoed. Cheery voices. A sales associate appeared with a man in plaid with rolled-up sleeves.

Plaid.

That got Sophie every time.

That man from church. Sophie had noticed him from time to time in the last six months since she had started attending Riverside Chapel. He would speak with her dad, but he hadn't once spoken to her.

Leonardo? Leo? Leon? What's his last name again?

For the life of her, she could not remember it, even after having read his contract with Simon's Gallery.

Whatever his name was, he had sung during the offertory. Maybe once or twice.

Standing there now, under the gallery lighting, he looked like he was in his late twenties or early thirties. He wasn't too tall, but his slightly disheveled hair might have added an inch to his height. His faded denim looked worn. He was wearing flip-flops.

He made a beeline for the pots and pans.

"Wonderful. *The Kitchen* has remained intact. I wasn't sure if it held. Part of it fell off in transit." He walked around his artwork and stopped in front of Baxter and Sophie.

"So, Bax, my man, what did Simon say about this?" he asked enthusiastically. "He loves it, right?"

Baxter cleared his throat again.

"Sheryl, will you get Baxter some water, please?" Sophie waved to the sales associate who had arrived with Mr. Plaid.

5

The sales associate nodded and left for the gallery kitchen. *The real kitchen.*

"About Simon... Bad news." Baxter shook his head. "After you left yesterday morning, he walked outside with a customer, slipped on the cobblestone, and broke a leg—shinbone."

"Ouch."

"He's on painkillers and in a cast." Baxter pointed to Sophie. "Please meet Sophie Kowalski. She'll be ruining—I mean, running—this gallery until Simon gets well."

"We've seen each other at church, I think. Or I've seen her." The man wiped his palm on his jeans and stretched out his hand toward Sophie. "Leon Watts, artist."

Ah, Leon.

Leon smiled. He had pretty teeth.

Teeth? Pretty? What am I thinking?

Sophie gingerly shook his hand.

But Leon had a lot to say. "Glad to finally meet you. Your dad talked a lot about you, though you and I haven't spoken in church."

Why would Dad talk about me to him?

Sophie didn't know how to respond. "What did he say to you?"

His eyes were blue like the sky outside. With indoor lighting being what it was, Sophie suspected his eyes were even lighter outdoors.

"Well, your dad is very proud of you," Leon explained. "Called you his favorite daughter."

"I'm his only daughter."

"There you go." He chuckled. "I'll be praying for him. Please let him know that."

Sophie nodded.

"If there's anything I can do, let me know, okay?"

"Yes, there is something you can do," Sophie finally said.

"At your service, ma'am."

"About this..." Sophie walked back to the other mixed-media art. "This..."

She made gestures with her hands.

"*The Laundry*," Leon said. His eyes met hers again. His brows furrowed.

"It does not look like laundry."

"You have to imagine it."

"Imagination is overrated," Sophie snapped.

"What are you saying?"

"We can't display this."

Leon looked befuddled. Almost shocked. "Your dad signed the contract."

"You will be compensated."

"We agreed. The keyword is *shown*. My art pieces must be shown. It's pointless otherwise."

Pointless. Exactly.

"I'm sure Baxter here can give you the names of

other galleries you can haul these to."

"Haul? We signed the contract," he repeated.

Everyone is repeating today.

"We display art pieces at our own discretion," Sophie reminded him. "It's on page four of the contract you signed."

"So you read it."

"Yes. I read everything." Sophie wasn't a technical writer for nothing. She knew she had an eye for details—words on paper in fine print—though at some point in time she had to rise above writing user guides and manuals for heavy machinery.

Still, they paid the bills, and she didn't have to borrow from Dad for mortgages or car payments. She'd like to think that her four-year English degree had worked out for her.

"I've made a total of twenty pieces to be rotated through the next ten days." Leon's voice was almost pleading.

Sophie hated to hear such a sad puppy voice.

"I've devoted a considerable amount of time to this *Home Life* series."

I wish he'd stop. "Hence, the compensation."

"That means nothing to me. I need the exposure. The discoverability. Visibility."

"That's why I asked Baxter to give you some contact names. I'm sure other galleries would be more than happy to display these."

"Your dad said he liked all my art pieces. I showed him videos of how I put them together."

"My dad and I have different tastes."

Leon folded his arms across his chest. There were paint streaks of different colors on both of his elbows.

"You have paint on your elbows," Sophie said.

"I'm an artist."

"Don't you want to wash off the paint?"

"No." Leon stood his ground. "What I want to know is this. Miss Sophie—I assume you're unmarried—are you prejudiced against the freedom of expression?"

CHAPTER TWO

*W*ell, *poor choice of words.*

Leon Watts couldn't take any of them back now. The words had gone out, splattered all over the gallery wall, and killed any hope of ever showcasing his sculpture or mixed-media artwork in Simon's Gallery.

He watched Sophie strut away, her heels clicking against the gallery floor.

What caught his attention was not her honey-blonde hair but her two-piece beige outfit that matched her equally beige leather pumps. They looked like a living blank canvas ready for him to paint bright strokes of colors on them.

Just because.

Maybe bright purple, the color of last night's sunset over Tybee Island.

Or this morning's sky across the Savannah River —the color of rust or yellow ochre—he couldn't decide which would better cover her shoes.

Shoes?

I want to paint her shoes?

Leon laughed. There was no way he would go ten feet near that woman. Dull and unimaginative.

"You'd better apologize to her, or we could both lose our jobs," Baxter said.

"I've already lost the contract, it seems. What good would it do?"

Leon glanced over to the front door. Sheryl was unlocking it. Outside the glass doors, pedestrians and tourists crisscrossed the sidewalk.

No one came in.

Just as well.

"When Simon comes back—and we expect a full recovery—you don't want him to hold it against you."

"I see."

"She's probably in Simon's office," Baxter added. "You've been there before."

Leon nodded. He hated to grovel. But the rent was due. His old van needed a new belt.

Simon Kowalski had given him his only chance all year long to make a scene.

And some scene he had made this morning, not the kind he had expected.

If he couldn't make a living as an artist, he had to get yet another job. That job at Piper's Place wouldn't be enough. He could ask for a second shift, but it meant he would work through the night, get five hours off, then go back to the restaurant for his day shift.

There'd be no time left for him to work on his artistic endeavors.

Yep. He had to get past that art-hater.

What was her name again?

He sighed, dug his hands into his jeans pocket, and made his way down the hallway toward Simon's office, where he hoped to find her to make amends.

～

Sophie closed her eyes and leaned back against the office chair as she listened on the phone to her stepmother's report on Dad's progress—or lack thereof.

She chuckled when Xian complained that Dad had insisted she wheel him to the gallery so he could get to work. Xian had promptly given him his pain medication, which put him out.

Sophie could barely hear the rest as she slowly fell asleep, holding the phone to her ear.

A loud crash woke her up.

She could hear Xian going, "Hello? Hello?"

Startled, Sophie sat up in the chair, held her forehead, and tried to regain her bearings.

Okay. I'm in...?

She winced. Reopened her eyes. Stared at the cluttered desk in front of her.

This is not my desk.

I'm not in my home office.

A hand—that looked like it belonged to a man—appeared in front of her, palm opened, her pink cell phone on top of it. It was cracked on one edge. It must have slipped out of her hand and onto the floor.

"Sophie? You there?" Xian's voice came out of the phone.

Sophie took the phone from the outstretched hand. Lifted it to her ear. Shut her eyes. "I'm here."

"I'll let you go, dear," her stepmother said. "You get some sleep, okay? Come over later, after work or something."

"I can stop by around lunch time."

"Your dad wouldn't want that. He'll think nobody's at the gallery."

"Baxter and Sheryl are here."

"You know how your dad is."

Yeah. Control freak. "Tell him I'll be eating lunch at his desk and working all day long."

"Good. See you at dinner? I'm cooking chicken."

Always chicken.

"Sure. Want me to bring something?" *You know, like beef.*

"Nah. I have everything. Just come. Bring a friend, if you like."

"A friend?" Sophie asked. She felt a headache coming.

"Preferably a boyfriend. Husband material."

"Husband what?" Sophie's head throbbed. She opened her eyes.

And there, standing in front of her, was Mr. Plaid.

"I've got to go. Someone's here to see me. Business." She emphasized *business*, for good measure.

Before her stepmother could ask if the visitor was a man or woman, Sophie bade her a hasty goodbye and hung up.

She drew in a deep breath.

Looked up.

"May I help you?" *No, I don't want to help you.*

Leon smiled. "I'm here to apologize for what I said to you out there. I overstepped. Wasn't my place to question your artistic preferences."

"I'm sorry?" A mind fog swept through Sophie's head.

Leon tilted his head. "When was the last time you slept?"

"Huh?"

"Baxter said ya'll stayed all night at the hospital with your dad. Did you get any shut-eye in the waiting room?"

"Uh..."

"I think the answer is no. Follow me." Leon stretched out his hand to help Sophie out of the chair.

"Maybe I shouldn't have sat down. I wouldn't have gone to sleep."

"On the other hand, there's a reason God gives us night."

"True." Sophie realized that Leon still had not let go of her hand. His hand was warm.

Is this how an artist's hand feels?

Leon led her to the end of the hallway. Inside a large storage room, were framed art pieces, sculptures, and all sorts of displays that Dad rotated through every week.

For the most part, this was Baxter's domain, but truth be told, Dad would have preferred to be both owner and director and manager and bookkeeper and everything.

Dad would have let Baxter go a long time ago if not for Dad's year-round allergies causing him to sometimes miss work. Baxter had filled in for Dad during those sick days. He had become invaluable.

For now.

Sophie wondered if Baxter had thought of

greater things. This was such a small local gallery, that the gallery manager's eye for art was poorly used. He was destined for a bigger art gallery, maybe a place in Atlanta or some bigger city. Or even that art museum several blocks away in historic Savannah.

Why am I even thinking of Baxter? "I need some sleep."

"Yes, you do. And I know just the solution so you don't have to drive in your condition." Leon led her to a corner of the cluttered storage room.

He let go of her hand.

Sophie felt wanting.

Leon lifted a canvas sheet over something rectangular.

Piled four feet high above something were quilts of all kinds. Crazy quilts, wedding-band quilts, postage-stamp quilts, all kinds. Old and worn, torn and restitched together. All kinds.

They reminded Sophie of visiting her grandmother's house in the foothills of the North Georgia Mountains, back in the days when Grandma had been alive and quilting.

"What is this? *Laundry, the Sequel?*" Sophie asked.

Without a word, Leon pulled off all the quilts, dumping them on the floor.

As soon as Sophie saw it, she knew what it was.

She has seen it before in an army surplus store, when she had accompanied Dad there—back in the days when Dad used to take her brother hunting and fishing in the summertime. Sophie hadn't been interested in those outdoor activities, preferring an air-conditioned room, thank you very much.

With a big sigh, Sophie kicked off her pumps and tried to climb onto the old army cot.

"Wait a minute. Not ready," Leon said.

Sophie waited as he put the quilts back on the cot, layering them one on top of another. After about ten layers, Sophie climbed in.

She was surprised that the quilts smelled of green fields. "Sunshine and the outdoors."

"Right. I laundered the quilts, and hung them outside to dry in the sun," Leon explained.

"Why?"

"This art exhibit is called *More Laundry*."

Sophie closed her eyes as her entire body rested on the stack of old quilts. "It's positively comfortable."

"I know."

As Sophie curled up on her side, she felt another quilt float on top of her...

CHAPTER THREE

*D*ad and Xian lived ten minutes away from the art gallery, in a three-story townhouse the size of three stacked shipping containers.

Or so it seemed.

Sophie parked her car on the street two blocks around the corner, in front of what used to be a carriage house back in the nineteenth century. Parking was free here after five, especially on a Tuesday. Tourists and out-of-towners usually started pouring into Savannah toward the weekend. The fireworks on Fridays were a big draw.

It was pushing six o'clock, and she was hungry for dinner. At this point she didn't care what kind of chicken dish Xian cooked.

If it wasn't chicken tonight, Sophie decided she'd take them out to eat next Friday.

Her phone rang as she turned the corner to find Dad's garage door open. The air was filled with the smell of something burning.

Jasmine rice.

She checked her phone. Jarvis from work. Well, not exactly from her office, but they had worked together numerous times when his company had hired her to update all their technical manuals on their tractor line. Jarvis was the manager that Sophie answered to. He had been nice to her, inviting her to their office parties and giving her an enviable office space in their company headquarters.

Some might say it was an overkill. She was only the technical writer, after all. A contract worker who was not on the employee payroll.

Still, the perks were nice. Free lunches in their lunchroom. Free coffee. Free cookies.

Then again, it had to come with a price, yes? How long could Sophie keep turning down Jarvis's offer to take her out to dinner?

The phone rang again.

Sophie almost took the call, when she heard sharp exchanges coming through the open door. Someone screaming and yelling.

Jarvis would have to wait.

Gingerly Sophie stepped between Dad's SUV

and his wall of tools, toward the kitchen door. The dreaded sounds of a quarrel grew louder.

Bracing herself, Sophie stepped onto ground zero.

She followed the noise to the living room, where Dad was lying down, moaning like he had broken something more than a shinbone.

The master bedroom was upstairs, but Dad couldn't climb the stairs at this time. Maybe he didn't want to.

In any case, he was stretched out on a queen bed that Baxter and Sophie had dragged out of the guest room—because Dad wanted to watch the big-screen television while recovering, and it was easier to move a bed to the living room than to relocate the wall-mounted TV to the bedroom.

Besides, it was only for about twelve weeks before Dad would be fully recovered.

Xian, his wife, was in an armchair.

She was crying. Dad was crying.

"What in the world is going on?" Sophie put down her keys, phone, and purse on a coffee table that had been moved to the side.

Playing arbitrator from time to time, Sophie knew what was coming. Still, she had to hear it. "Who gets to go first?"

Xian pointed an accusing finger at Dad. "He needs to go back to work. Pronto! He's a poor patient. Very poor. Complaining all the time. Did I say all the time? The room is too hot, too cold, too this, too that. Waiting on him, I forgot all about the rice I was cooking on the stove. Dinner is ruined!"

"It's not my fault the fire alarm went off," Dad said.

Xian dabbed her eyes with wet wads of tissue paper. "I can't stand it anymore. Either he goes back to work, or I'm moving out."

"That's a good idea actually—"

"What?"

"No, no. I mean, me going back to work, dear."

"Oh, you were going to say I should move out!" Xian wailed.

"I didn't! I'm saying someone has to run the gallery."

Sophie stepped between them. "I'm running the gallery. Remember, Dad? You put me in charge. Gave me all sorts of authority."

"I was heavily medicated."

"The gallery is fine. Nothing to worry about." Sophie decided she'd tell them later how she had slept all through lunch and half the afternoon on Leon's cot in the gallery's back room, but they didn't have to know. Besides, Baxter had covered for her.

"We just got home from the hospital this morning." Sophie stared at the clock. "So we're talking no more than twelve hours, and you're having cabin fever already, Dad?"

Dad didn't say anything.

"He's a control freak," Xian said.

"Your doctor said you need to rest," Sophie reminded Dad. "It'll take weeks for you to heal. Either heal now, or suffer later."

Dad glared at her. "I'm fine."

"Only because you're on pain meds. When they wear off, you're going to feel your leg."

"So what do we do?" Xian asked. Her voice sounded desperate.

"This is your staycation," Sophie announced. "How about this? In the morning I'll bring you a laptop. We'll put a live cam in the gallery, and you can see all that's going on. Text me and tell me what to do, and it will be done."

Dad's eyes lit up. "I like that idea."

Sophie knew Dad well. He was a hands-on CEO. He wasn't even a super fan of art. To Dad, Simon's Gallery was a business for profit and a way to give back to the community. If someone offered to buy the gallery at the right price, Dad would sell the place in a heartbeat.

Every now and then, Dad would float the idea of moving out west to somewhere drier, like Arizona —where Sophie's older brother lived. Every year Dad's allergies were getting less seasonal and more year round. Even without the broken leg, Dad had enough problems with pollen and cut grass and the humid southern climate.

For now he had to live with it.

"I'll send a message to Baxter to install live cams in the gallery. He'll have to figure out how to get it done between now and tomorrow." Sophie retrieved her phone from her purse and tapped away.

Dad was visibly excited. "I want to see patrons' faces when they see Leon's *Home Life* series."

Uh-oh. "Ah, about that…"

"Leon delivered all the pieces on time, didn't he?" Dad asked.

"Yeah, but…"

"There's not enough room? I cleared some space in the back for him."

Sophie had to tell him. There was nothing else she could do about it. "I canceled the exhibit."

"You what?" Dad's jaw dropped to his chest.

"You said I could do what I think is best."

"The painkiller said that. I didn't." Dad pointed to Sophie's phone. "Call him back."

"The contract said it would be at our discretion."

"Last time I checked, I still own the gallery."

"You told me I could make decisions." He did too! Sophie wasn't sure whether to feel angry or upset or both. There was no way she was going to have any of Leon's stuff in the gallery, not while she was in charge.

"Not Leon's art. You leave that to me."

"You didn't say—"

"I must've forgotten. Leon is like a son to me."

Seriously? "I asked Baxter to make some calls. A gallery in Charleston might be interested in some of his disturbing—uh...art."

"I like them. I want them in Simon's Gallery. Find a way, Sophie."

Her businessman dad baffled her sometimes. Sophie realized then that she really didn't know Dad that well if she didn't know his taste anymore.

"What's there now?" Dad asked, his voice low, indicating that something was brewing.

"Tina MacFarland's pottery."

Dad nodded. "How long?"

"One week."

"That's not enough time."

"For what?" Sophie asked.

Xian cut in. "For the next-door building to be ready to show."

Sophie had completely forgotten about the foreclosure purchase of the old store next door to Simon's Gallery. The combined space would more than double the size of the gallery.

It made sense to put some out-of-kilter artwork, sculpture, and mixed-media art there.

"We could dedicate one of the floors entirely to modern art," Xian suggested. "Leon's pots and pans would be happy there."

Happy?

Pots and pans?

Before Sophie could say a word, Dad beamed. "You're marvelous. I love you." He stretched his working arm toward his wife.

Xian went to him and kissed him on the forehead. "Even if I burned the rice?"

"I don't care as long as you're with me."

Xian smiled. "I guess you can stay in the house until you feel better, Mr. Kowalski."

"Why, thank you, Mrs. Kowalski."

And Sophie rolled her eyes.

"Well, I'm glad. Dad can't stay with me. My townhouse is even smaller than this." When Sophie had bought her own place, she had been happy to have her own space. However, as the years had worn on, the small space crowded her in.

A tiny one-bedroom townhouse for one.

In the beginning, it had felt cozy. Nowadays, Sophie felt shortsighted with her purchase as she watched her friends get married and move into family-size houses, pair by pair.

And here she was, alone.

Keeping busy was her way of dealing with loneliness. A workaholic streak ran in the Kowalski family, and that had been her saving grace.

But, God, please. I don't want to be lonely anymore.

Maybe she should go out once in a while.

Well, first, someone had to invite her out.

Jarvis had.

Sophie groaned.

"Sophie?" Dad asked. "What's wrong?"

"Ah. Nothing. So can I help with dinner or something?" she asked.

Xian threw up her arms. "I'm still on strike, in spite of everything."

"I'll cook," Sophie offered.

"I already threw out the pot with the burned rice in it."

"Okay." Sophie tried to think of something. "Maybe we won't cook tonight. Let the poor kitchen rest? How about if I order out? We can get a delivery."

"That's too expensive," Dad said.

"It's on me." Sophie smiled. "A get-well-soon dinner."

"Nice. Do we get a cheesecake with it? I think that'll help me recover."

"Anything you want."

Anything you want.

Sophie wondered if she could wish that for

herself. Some excitement to her life. Some adventure perhaps?

Then again, an all-wise God wouldn't give her everything she wanted. She could ruin her life on account of it.

Yes, even at twenty-nine years old, she could still ruin her life.

Better stay on the safe road.

CHAPTER FOUR

*E*veryone was too busy to make it to the occasional women's dinner before the midweek service except Sophie, Heidi Wei, Nadine Saylor, and Abilene Dupree.

But sitting alone, Sophie wondered if any of those friends from Riverside Chapel would come at all.

Actually, Nadine and Abilene almost couldn't make it, as they were busy with other things. Abilene had just graduated from the Savannah College of Art and Design, and she designed their church programs, brochures, handouts, you name it.

She's an artist.

Maybe she could do something for Simon's Gallery, help increase the income.

The thought rang in Sophie's mind as she

waited at Piper's Place for the women to show up. Sophie looked through the window to the late-afternoon sky above the waterfront and the river.

River Street was busy with people everywhere. Mostly tourists, as per usual. Some were pouring into Piper's Place. It made Sophie glad that she had made a reservation.

With all those tourists going through Savannah every year, Sophie wondered why in the world was Dad's art gallery not doing as well as he had thought?

Sophie had looked at the numbers in the accounting software. Dad had managed the accounting himself, but the receipts showed that a lot of his art displays hadn't sold in the last twelve months.

That had been the primary reason Sophie was insistent on not showing artwork that couldn't sell.

Once they took care of the mold problem in the next-door space that Dad had bought, putting more displays there seemed counterintuitive to Sophie. After all, while many people went through art galleries, those who actually opened their checkbooks and bought something would only be a small percentage of the number of visitors.

However, if Simon's Gallery added an educational angle...

Dad had friends in the Savannah Senior Living

Resort. Perhaps some of the retirees there might want to take art classes?

Now why hadn't Dad thought of that?

Sophie felt odd that she had come up with that possible income-increasing option for Simon's Gallery.

Lord Jesus, You must have given me that idea. I'm not creative enough.

Even as she said it in her heart, Sophie wondered if it was true.

Am I really not creative, or have I just not exercised creativity as much as artists have—artists such as Leon?

Noisy keys made Sophie look away from the window.

Heidi Wei slid into the bench across from her. "Sorry. My project meeting at school ran late a bit."

"Not to worry. Compared to Nadine and Abilene, we're both sort of early," Sophie said.

The server came, and they both ordered water.

"How's your dad doing?" Heidi asked.

"Coming along. He doesn't want to be sitting at home doing nothing."

"I hear you. At least ten people signed up for meals. Three are bringing their covered dishes tonight, and we're spreading out the rest for the next two Sundays."

Sophie didn't know what to say. She sniffled. "That's very kind of you."

"Least we can do." Heidi surveyed the menu. "I always get the same things here. What are you having?"

"Just a salad."

"On a diet?"

"No appetite."

"Worried about something?"

"Maybe. Just that I'm not cut out to run the gallery, but until Dad gets better, he wants me to do it. Why would he ask me, a technical writer, to help him manage an art gallery?"

"Ah, a puzzle. Are you sort of in between work?"

"No, but freelancing gives me flexible hours, so I simply cleared my calendar for two months to do this for Dad."

"He's paying you?"

"Yep. He's just paying me by the hour. Same rate as what he paid me when he needed me to write brochures for the gallery. The only difference is that he put me in charge of his gallery."

"I didn't know you're into art."

"Well, I used to follow him around on my summer breaks in high school and college when he made acquisitions for the galleries he worked for.

Now that job's done by Baxter. I just sit in Dad's office to make his presence known."

"Still a job."

"Right."

"Can you do it though? Is it up your alley?"

"Art is not really my thing, but since I manage my own business, I know what a bottom line looks like." Sophie wondered how far to go.

Could she trust her friend?

She decided she could. "It's an art gallery. It has overhead. I can tell you that a lot of the commissioned works are not selling. Even with tourists flocking here, not everyone is looking for a three-thousand-dollar painting, you know?"

Heidi nodded.

"And then just before Dad broke his leg, he bought the shop next door. Perfect timing."

"More mortgages." Heidi shook her head.

"It gets worse. They gutted it and found mold."

"No way."

"Unfortunately, when it rains..." Sophie almost laughed. It wasn't funny, but it was sad the way costs accumulated.

"We'll pray for God's perfect will to be done," Heidi said.

"Thank you."

Their orders came. Heidi asked Sophie to say a

blessing. She made it quick, but there was so much she wanted to pray about.

"So the gallery needs income," Heidi said.

"Yeah. I'm thinking of suggesting that the space next door be used for art education."

"You should ask Abilene."

"I was just thinking of her. But I don't know her very well." Sophie poured salad dressing over the pile of greens. She should have asked for chicken or beef to go with it, but she hadn't thought of all that when they were ordering. She was usually more thorough than this, but there had been so much on her mind lately.

"I'll ask her for you, if you just let me know when. She's in her last year of art school. She could possibly recommend some other SCAD graduates who stay in town."

"Thanks." Sophie waved to their server.

"And there's Leon from church," Heidi added. "He could teach too."

Leon.

"I had to tell Leon that his mixed-media artwork won't work in our gallery," Sophie said.

She didn't tell Heidi that the gallery needed something else that sold faster.

"Leon's a good guy."

"Glad to hear that. Maybe he won't be too upset that I told him to take his art pieces elsewhere."

"In those words?" Heidi's eyes were big.

"Politely, of course."

"Of course." Heidi's phone buzzed. She checked the screen. "Nadine can't make it again. That girl works entirely too much. Abilene is on her way."

"Please don't mention the art class idea yet, okay?" Sophie said. "I need to discuss it with Dad first, and he hasn't been in the mood. I didn't want him to get a blood clot or something when I tell him that his bookkeeping is poor, at best."

"Gotcha. Mum's the word. But I'll be praying." Heidi pointed a fork at her. "Something else on your mind?"

Something else? "Like what else?"

"You tell me. You seem a bit pensive."

Sophie drew a deep breath. "Someone from work—well, a client who hires me to write manuals —asked me out to dinner."

"And?"

"I've turned him down so many times that I felt sorry for him. He keeps coming back. So I was thinking, maybe just one dinner."

"In a public place, of course."

"Like here." Sophie figured that if anything happened at dinner, she could leave. "I'll drive my own car."

"I'll pray for you. You don't have to go out to dinner with anyone you don't like."

"It's not that I don't like him, but I hate to mix business with pleasure, you know." As soon as she spoke it, Sophie spotted Leon talking with customers at another table.

He looked great in plaid.

Heidi seemed to notice. She glanced. "I didn't know Leon works here."

"Neither did I."

"Must've just started since the last time I was here," Heidi added. "He's a cutie."

Sophie nodded.

"You nodded!" Heidi laughed.

CHAPTER FIVE

*T*he day after Mom had paddled out to sea in the tropical storm, Leon had found a handwritten letter in her Bible, tucked between the books of Exodus and Leviticus.

If the placement had meant anything, it was lost to Leon.

The letter had simply—and clinically—stated that she had gone to *swim with the dolphins.*

It's easier this way; no one needs to pay for a burial plot.

The semicolon had gotten to Leon first. Once a writer, always a writer?

Even this early morning, barely at sunrise, sitting on the sandy beach and looking out at the

Atlantic Ocean, Leon dared not say that his mom's failed attempt to be noticed by big-name publishers had caused her downward spiral.

No, she had been this way since Leon had been born. Her husband had walked out on the young mother even before she had weaned Leon. Jobless and on welfare, she had ended up working odd jobs here and there.

Twenty-some years later, nothing had changed except that Mom had sunk deeper and deeper into regrets and remorse and landfills of unfulfilled dreams.

Whom could he blame?

Leon wiped a stray tear from his eye. He looked up at the morning sky. He had thought it was going to rain. Nope. Not a single droplet from the sky.

Must be sand and wind in his eye.

He blinked.

Leon stared ahead at the calm sea that had buried so many.

Two days after he had discovered Mom's note in the Bible—a note that had been addressed to no one, not even her only child—he had made an abrupt decision to leave the country.

Was I being Jonah, Lord?

Did I run away?

He had told the then-pastor of Riverside Chapel —it had been before Pastor Diego Flores had been called—that he had to find international inspiration for his artwork.

It hadn't been exactly the truth, but no one had questioned him when he used artistic expression as a reason to do the irrational, like travel through the Southern Hemisphere for eighteen months until his savings account was depleted.

Reality had been more stark.

Leon had been upset that Mom had left him alone, that she had not waited for her natural end, that she had taken matters into her own hands.

"Why didn't You stop her, Lord?" Leon barely whispered into the whipping wind.

The sun was rising, but Leon remained seated on the packed sand as people with their morning coffee and dogs on leashes walked around him, being careful not to obstruct his view.

He was two hours early for the meeting with the rental manager, but he had to see that house on the beach that Mom had wanted to live in for the longest time but never had the chance.

It was finally for rent.

Two years too late for Mom.

Leon was determined to rent it in her memory.

It was the least he could do to say goodbye to her.

He wasn't due for work at Piper's Place until eleven o'clock. It was a chore to work from eleven to eleven, but such was life. He couldn't imagine what it was like to have to do menial work for twenty years, but Mom had done it to feed him.

Public school had been free, so that was that. State-sponsored meals after school had helped stave off his hunger on most days. All in all, he and Mom had been dirt poor all their lives.

And now he had chosen the worst profession to make a living with. Yes, some had succeeded as money-making artists, but most of the time, he had been starving, and that hadn't been a cliché.

If not for his job at Piper's Place, he'd be on welfare.

Just like Mom had been before him.

Truly, Mom had been given only six months to live.

"So why didn't she ride it out? Why, Lord?"

The doctor had said there was a two percent chance she could beat the brain cancer, but the tumor was inoperable.

Two percent.

Is our God not the God of the impossible?

Why did Mom give up?

Why, Mom? Why?

Often, in his travels through Asia, Australia, and New Zealand, and then Chile and Argentina, Leon had blamed himself. Perhaps if he hadn't gone away to bigger cities to sell his folk art, then he could have done more—way more!—to help Mom through her deep depression.

A sharp buzz from his phone jolted him.

He checked.

The rental manager had arrived and was waiting for him at the front driveway of the house he wanted to rent for his living quarters and art studio. He had parked his car there, and had walked here.

He texted back that he'd be there in a couple of minutes, all the time wondering how on earth he was going to pay for the rent if Simon's Gallery had just axed his exhibition.

That woman!

Leon was surprised he wasn't angry with Sophie Kowalski at all. Instead, he felt drawn to her somehow, in spite of what she had done to his livelihood. By canceling his *Home Life* exhibition at the gallery, Sophie had effectively ensured that he could not pay his rent for the next six months.

And yet.

Yet he wasn't mad at her.

He had seen her sleep deprived the other day, and had let her nap in one of his exhibition pieces. He wouldn't have done that had he been upset with her.

Why? He had no idea.

*F*riday night was the worst night to be eating at Piper's Place. Without a reservation, the wait had been unbearably long. The crowd was noisy. The music loud. The air stifling.

All Sophie wanted to do even now, when they were finally seated, was to run out of here and go home.

The lack of planning told her to cross Jarvis off the list of dates. Mentally, she put him under *do not respond.*

She probably shouldn't have agreed to dinner with him considering that he was a business associate and all. It was going to be awkward the next time his company hired her to update their tractor user guide.

At first Sophie and Jarvis had sat on opposite ends of the booth.

Then, for some reason, Jarvis decided he wanted to sit on the same side as Sophie.

She found that too close for comfort and tried to ask him to scoot out and go back to the other side.

He refused.

Instead, he leaned over and pecked her on the cheek.

She pushed him away.

Is anybody watching? I need some help here.

Not understanding what she meant, Jarvis

leaned toward her again and—horrors!—nibbled her ear.

"No! Stop!" What else could she have said?

Jarvis must not have heard her.

Yeah, right. Two inches away?

"Get you something?" A third voice interrupted them. A harsh voice.

Leon.

He was wearing a Piper's Place apron. And that plaid shirt again. He was holding a pitcher of water or tea or something cold. Sophie could see the condensation on the outside of the stainless-steel wall.

Then, nonchalantly, he tilted the pitcher.

Ice and water splashed onto Jarvis's arm and down the front of his shirt and pants. He yelped and lurched out of his seat, expletives pouring out of his mouth.

"Oh sorry." Leon's voice was unreadable, but his face...

He looked positively furious.

Since Jarvis was no longer blocking her seat, Sophie grabbed her purse and slipped out of the booth.

By then the manager was there, talking to Jarvis, trying to calm him down.

Sophie dashed for the door. Someone reached around her and opened it for her.

Leon.

Her rescuer.

Again.

"How are you getting home?" His voice was low.

"I drove here myself."

"Good for you." He seemed relieved. "I was going to offer you a ride home."

"You're working."

"My shift is almost over—well, in two hours, but I can get someone to cover for me." Leon ushered her outside. "Let me walk you to your car."

"Thank you." And Sophie meant it.

CHAPTER SIX

*I*t was raining heavily at nine o'clock when Baxter parked his car to let Sophie out at the front door of the big house that looked like it could be carried off by the ocean in a severe hurricane. Hurricane season was coming soon. This early-October rain couldn't compete with the gale-force winds.

"Go on," Baxter said, putting on the parking brakes. He swiped his cell phone.

"You're not going in?" Sophie asked.

"Not in this rain. I'll just wait here where it's nice and dry. I've got lots of emails to write and phone calls to return. Text me if you want me to see some art pieces that we might want to show." Baxter laughed.

"Don't get hit by lightning," Sophie said.

"If it gets too bad, I'll go inside."

"Good."

"You two are adults, so I'm not worried. I can chaperone from here."

Sophie rolled her eyes. She wondered what Dad would think if he had heard what Baxter just said.

Does a twenty-eight-year-old woman need a chaperone?

Still, she struggled out of the vehicle, wondering if she should have suggested coming here at all.

Well, she had to come.

Still, she stood outside the car, holding her gift box under an umbrella and wondering if she should even knock on the door, let alone go inside. Before she could decide to get back into the car, the front door opened, and there was Leon Watts, in a plaid shirt.

A different one this time.

He motioned for her to come inside.

Oh well.

Sophie sloshed her way to the front door. Leon took the umbrella from her and shook it out. He squinted his eyes and seemed to be trying to look through the rain.

"Is someone else in the car?" he asked.

"Baxter."

"He drove you here?"

"I asked him to." Might as well tell him she had

no design. Perhaps this trip had been poorly planned. Too late now.

"Oh. He's not coming in?"

Sophie shook her head. "Unless the storm gets worse."

Leon leaned the umbrella in an old umbrella stand just inside the front door. "What brings you here, Miss Sophie?"

"I brought you a thank-you gift." Sophie handed him the box. It had a pretty ribbon on top.

"Aww. For what?"

"You know." Sophie watched him stare at the box. "Open it."

He did. "How do you know I'm not allergic to chocolate?"

"Are you?" She hoped not, because it was the only unopened box of chocolate she had left in her house.

"I'm allergic to *not* having any chocolate." Leon ushered her to what could have been a living room once upon a time. Now it was stripped bare to the studs. In the middle of it were lots of boxes.

Sophie didn't even want to ask what mixed media Leon was working on.

He pulled up a folding chair. "Have a seat?"

After Sophie did, Leon offered her the chocolate. "Ladies first."

"Or you're testing to see if these are poisoned."

"What?"

"Just making a joke."

He didn't say anything. He sat down on the floor.

Sophie realized that Leon had given her the only chair he had.

"These are delicious." Leon smiled. "Thank you. So it was worth all that trouble last night."

"You could have been fired."

"You were violated. He was in your personal space." His eyes grew angry and dark again. "You should press charges. I'm not the only witness."

"No?"

"No. In fact, I didn't notice you were there until another server told me that your dad was going to beat up that jerk."

"He would, yes." Sophie's voice cracked. "Let's not talk about him anymore."

"I gather he's off the list."

"He was never on the list. Just a business associate wanting dinner."

"Right. Don't defend him, Sophie. He's no good for you."

"Thank you for coming to my assistance." Sophie meant it.

Leon opened his mouth.

"No," Sophie said.

"No what? What was I going to say?"

"I still can't let you display your junk—art—in Dad's gallery."

Leon shook his head. "I was only trying to say that any server at Piper's Place would have come to your aid. Sometimes we have people so drunk they have no idea what they were doing. We call a cab for them, you know."

"Right. Sorry."

"Don't worry about it."

Silence.

Sophie felt a need to explain. "I've known him from various projects we've done, but it was the first time we went out away from work."

"So he thought his association with you gave him the license to do as he pleased."

"I don't know. Men are..."

Leon stared at her. "Men? All men? You were saying?"

"I was going to say I don't get men."

Leon laughed. "What fun would there be if you *got* us?"

"It's hard to find someone who..." Sophie sighed. "Do you date?"

She didn't know why she asked.

Leon didn't say anything at first.

"Sometimes," he finally said. "Not lately. I can't afford it. Have to pay the rent and buy more garbage —literally."

Sophie laughed. "Garbage?"

"That's what you think of my *Home Life* exhibition, yes?" Leon's eyebrows rose.

"I'm sorry." Sophie glanced at the pile of boxes in the middle of the room. If they caught on fire... "I didn't appreciate what you were doing."

"And you do now?"

"Not really."

"Figured." He got up from the floor, handed Sophie the rest of the chocolate, and walked toward the boxes. Pointed to them. "What do you see?"

"A fire hazard."

"Oh, very good." Leon turned serious. "*Moving Day*."

"Is that the name of this display?"

Leon nodded. "You don't see it."

"I'm trying to understand."

"Me or my art?"

Sophie shrugged. "Well, both, I think."

CHAPTER SEVEN

*L*eon gently pulled Sophie to her feet.

Under normal circumstances, she would've considered the gesture too forward. Yet for some reason, she felt at ease with Leon. He seemed safe. Besides, Baxter was sitting in the car outside the house, ready to drive her home. It wasn't like they had enough time for anything inappropriate to happen.

"I see treasure. You see trash." Leon walked her around the pile of boxes in the middle of the room. "I see gold. You see garbage."

"Nice alliterations."

"A what?"

"Never mind. Go on." Sophie followed him to another end of the room, where a door led to another room.

"Does anyone else live here?" Sophie asked. "I saw the *For Rent* signs out on the street."

"I'm the only one here for now. They let me use the downstairs rooms to put my art, but as soon as there are other tenants, I have to find somewhere else to store them."

"So why not rent an art studio?"

"I wanted to, but the landlady was desperate to have tenants here, so she gave me a deal. I pay month to month, and I can leave any time if I find a better place." Leon dropped Sophie's hand. "I'm sorry. I didn't realize I was still holding your hand."

"I didn't either."

"Glad to know I'm non-threatening," Leon said.

"Dad trusts you."

"He does?" His face grew bright.

"I got an earful after I told him I replaced your artwork."

Leon leaned toward Sophie. "I want to believe that you came here to see me, to tell me you changed your mind about letting me put my art in your gallery—and maybe even add them as a part of your permanent collection."

Sophie could barely breathe. "No—"

"I'm disappointed on behalf of all the artists in the world."

"You didn't let me finish."

"You said no."

"I did, but Dad's going to handle your...stuff—exhibition—here on out."

"Working from home?" Leon asked.

"You know my dad. He can never not work." Sophie hated to fish, but there it was. She wanted to know how well Leon knew her dad.

"Yeah. He'll probably work until the day he—ooh. I didn't mean that. You know what I meant."

"I guess. So you know my dad super well?"

"Only on Sundays." Leon waited and then asked, "How come our paths never crossed at church?"

"Is there a need?"

"Ah, life is not all about needs, is it?"

"What do you mean?"

"Sure, there are needs and wants, but life can be fun also."

"After you finish work."

"My work is fun," Leon countered. "I like my job."

"Good for you." Sophie's voice was tepid.

Do I like my job? Technical writing was precise and pedantic prose. Black and white. What you saw was what it needed to be. There was no creativity there, except perhaps a turn of words to make it even more defined and accurate.

As Sophie thought about her own career, Leon walked toward some sort of structure taller than himself. The drop cloth covering it was awash with multicolored paint.

"I'm in the middle of a new piece of art," Leon said. "Would you like to see it?"

"A sculpture?"

"Mixed media." His fingers held the edges of the drop cloth. He waited.

"Should I brace myself?" Sophie felt nervous.

Leon didn't say a word as he pulled down the drop cloth, revealing a giant cylindrical fish tank filled with women's shoes, sneakers, suitcases, books, spiral notebooks, printer paper—all painted over in neon colors. Sprinkled here and there were giant chunks of charcoal.

"Charcoal is not a neon color," Sophie said.

"Very good. It represents darkness."

"I get that." Sophie stepped back for a wider view. "Have you considered making smaller... uh...*structures*? This display would take up an enormous space. A smaller pile—I mean display—might get you into more galleries."

"Now that was an idea I haven't thought of," Leon said. "Anyway, guess what the title is."

"Landfill?"

Leon stopped smiling. "No."

"You asked me to guess."

"This is my mother's life," he said quietly.

"Your mom?" Sophie's palm flew to her lips. "I don't get it."

"One day, Mom was here in this very building, looking to rent an apartment—to where I could come home for Thanksgiving. She couldn't afford the rent. Two weeks later, she paddled out into the tropical storm."

"Was it an accident?"

"She knew the storm was coming."

"Oh." Sophie gasped. She reached for Leon. "Oh... So sorry."

Leon folded his arms. "I'm not looking for sympathy."

Sophie sensed a wall going up. She retracted her hand.

Without a word, Leon dragged an edge of the drop cloth, climbed up a ladder next to the fish tank, and covered his partially completed work.

Like a burial shroud, the drop cloth fell over the fish tank.

Leon climbed down the ladder, smiled to Sophie, and offered her another piece of chocolate.

CHAPTER EIGHT

"**S**o every artwork tells a story," Sophie concluded.

"Yes." Even as he said it, Leon wondered why he had to state the obvious. He found it hard to believe that Sophie lacked imagination. It had to be there.

Never used.

But it had to be there.

"Why didn't you say so back at the gallery on Tuesday?" Sophie asked.

"It's in the title."

"*The Laundry. The Kitchen.* Those tell me nothing."

"I'm not a writer." He paused. He wasn't sure how much more to say. "My mother was a writer, but I can't write to save my life."

"Maybe I can help," Sophie said. "I write user guides and manuals for a living."

"Yeah? What kind of user guides?" He could just imagine the plethora of user guides. He saw them all the time on the back side of microwaveable dinner boxes.

"For heavy farm equipment and factory machinery. That sort of thing."

"Well, okay. I guess a guide is a guide is a guide." Leon folded his arms again. He knew he was doing it a lot and hoped Sophie hadn't noticed. "I don't know how you can help me. I just need some sort of description for my artwork, right? In proper English, I suppose?"

"It doesn't have to be formal. It could be conversational. We could even record you."

"Oh no. My voice doesn't sound good on audio."

"How do you know that?"

"I'm an artist, not a narrator." Leon stood his ground.

"All right. So you tell me the story of each of your sculptures or mixed-media artwork, and I'll write it down for you. Maybe you can record yourself reading it aloud."

"All that sounds expensive." Leon shook his head. "I can't pay you. Why are you doing this?"

Sophie didn't reply.

"You feel sorry for me."

Sophie barely nodded.

"Then un-cancel our consignment contract."

Sophie didn't answer his request directly. "Did you call the gallery in Charleston?"

"Yes, but they don't have space until next year. I need income sooner." Leon felt strongly that he had to speak his mind. "You're afraid."

Sophie's jaw dropped. "Did you just accuse me of something?"

Leon was about to step into no-man's-land, but if he didn't go there, he'd never get his new series of artwork out for the public to see.

That half-day partial exhibition on Tuesday hadn't been enough.

Leon knew then that he had to expand his contacts. Reach out to more galleries. Maybe outside Savannah. Maybe even outside the state.

So here goes. "You're afraid, Miss Kowalski, that if you get to know my work more, you might actually like the stories I tell with my *Home Life* series."

"I disagree."

"Your opinion versus mine."

"If I were afraid, I wouldn't have come here at all. Brought you chocolate. Spent time alone with you in this house—whether Baxter was sitting outside or not. Let you show me your artwork."

"True. I have to agree with that. You could've

accused me of something. Brought charges against me. Ruined my career. Ruined my life."

"And why would I do that?"

Leon shrugged. "Who knows. I've always had a hard life. I kinda expect things."

"Expect things? Like bad things? What about God? Doesn't God give you good things?" Sophie waved her arms about. "A roof over your head. Food. Chocolate. Be thankful."

Be thankful.

"That's an advice I need to hear, badly." Leon glanced at an old clock on the wall. It was past ten o'clock. He had to leave at ten thirty if he wanted to be on time for work at Piper's Place.

Sophie must have noticed his concern. "What time do you have to leave for work?"

"In twenty minutes." Leon ushered her back to the foyer. "But I want to say that maybe God brought you here for such a time as this."

"For such a time as what?"

"I don't know." Leon was being honest. "To be revealed in due time, I guess. God's timing is perfect."

"Well, maybe God has also brought you here for such a time as this, Leon."

Leon opened the front door. The rain had stopped.

"Thank you for the chocolate." He handed Sophie her umbrella, still dripping wet.

"Thank you for the rescue."

"I hope I don't have to do it again."

"Ever."

CHAPTER NINE

*R*iverside Chapel had been meeting in this small upstairs office space that overlooked the Savannah River since they had formed a year ago. Leon Watts looked around and counted all the charter members here this morning, notably the Wei siblings, who had been the driving force behind this church plant.

Driving force? Perhaps that should have been credited to God instead.

True, Aidan Ming Wei and his sister, Heidi, had found out that their old friend, Diego Flores, who had been planting churches the last three years, had been looking for a new church to start or grow. His mission board had been taking requests.

However, it had been God who had brought the young and single Pastor Flores to Savannah.

It had also been God who had brought Leon here, for whatever reason.

Leon took his place at the back row, as per usual. He listened to the way the plastic folding chairs dragged on the old wooden floor as people came in and adjusted to their seats. He listened to the scratching noise. He listened to the way the sounds of wood mixed with the sounds of human voices.

And wondered if he could make a new sculpture out of that idea.

Yes, a sculpture this time.

If he kept piling things together with chicken-coop wire or putting them into glass tanks, Sophie would keep calling them junk.

Well, she hadn't exactly used that word, but he could read her mind.

Yeah? Could I?

Instinctively, his eyes looked around, his heart wondering.

Is Sophie here?

Simon Kowalski was a charter member of Riverside Chapel. His wife, Xian, was usually loud and had a hearty laughter. Sophie was the quiet one in the family.

That could explain why Leon hadn't noticed her much.

Her dad, on the other hand, had been busy

inviting his friends from the Savannah Senior Living Center to attend church at Riverside.

And his business associates, like that riverboat captain.

Speaking of whom, there he was, at the door.

The riverboat captain.

Leon couldn't remember his name now, but they had been praying for his salvation for a while. His daughter ran a walking-tour outfit in town. His wife had died of cancer a long time ago, which had been how he—ah, Jerome Pendegrast was his name!—had come to know Simon.

Simon had ministered to Jerome in the widower's grief since that time. According to Simon, Jerome was very close to salvation.

Very close, but not quite.

Leon sat alone. He wasn't sure why he hadn't just gone to the front to mix with the dozen people milling about and sitting closer to the pulpit.

Eventually he would. Pastor Flores had asked him to play the offertory today.

He felt a bit nervous. He hadn't picked up his guitar all week, until last night, when it had suddenly dawned on him that he was serving God this morning.

Is this how I serve God?

Shame on me.

There was nowhere to go. He should practice

more, but this was a simple piece. Mom had said that he was born to play music. He had picked up the guitar in elementary school and had taken free lessons from a retired musician down the street from the apartment complex where he and mom had lived, in exchange for mowing his lawn.

It had worked out.

When he had helped Mr. Stapleton clean his gutters, he would be allowed to play one of his Gibsons. Unfortunately, Mr. Stapleton had a heart attack before Leon finished high school. His children sold all his guitars.

"Thank you, Leon!" someone said.

Leon turned, lost in thought. He blinked the person into focus.

Aidan Ming Wei.

"Man, you're a lifesaver," Ming added. "If you had said no, we'd be doing a silent offertory this morning."

"No problem. How's your sister doing?"

"Sick as a puppy. She caught something on campus, and I think I'm going to get it from her. Hope it's not the flu."

"I hear you, man. Happy to help, and tell her she's on the prayer list."

Yes, among other duties—like filling in for soloists when they were too sick to sing offertories —Leon was also in charge of the prayer list for

Riverside Chapel. It was amazing that, for a new church with under fifty people, there had been many prayer requests in the last several months alone.

"Will do." Ming waved and left to talk to Pastor Flores.

When Leon looked their way, his gaze went past them to the exit. Somewhere in his heart, he hoped she would walk through the door.

She?

Yes, she.

Unfortunately, she did not. Instead, Leon spotted Xian Kowalski chatting away with her friends. That only meant Sophie would not be here this morning. She was probably taking care of her dad, who was on the prayer list.

Somehow, Leon felt disappointed.

CHAPTER TEN

*L*eon tossed a single stem of marigold into
the ebbing tide. The foam and salt water
carried the flower petals out to the expan-
sive ocean, to the deep beyond.

"Bye, Mom." His whisper choked in the
Atlantic breeze and sputtered away toward the
morning sun.

"Lord, I turn her over to you."

*How many times have I done that in the last two
years?*

And yet again, another final hour, another goodbye. This time he had brought Mom's favorite
flower.

"Lord, please tell Mom that I'm staying in the
house she wanted to rent. If all goes well, I'll have
Thanksgiving here and think of her."

He didn't think anyone else walking about could hear him, because the noise of surf and gulls would mask his anguish, so he continued.

Tried to.

"Tell her not to worry about me. I'll be fine."

Leon remembered Sophie's words. "What about God? Doesn't God give you good things?"

Ah, yes, good things.

"A roof over your head. Food. Chocolate. Be thankful."

Be thankful.

"Thank You, Lord, for Mom, her memories, her legacy." Leon lifted his face to the sky, closed his eyes, and let the salty wind and eastern sun spray his face.

He stood there for the longest time, until he was suddenly aware that he had to eat some breakfast and then rush to Piper's Place for the lunch shift. He was getting tired of waiting tables, but grateful that Piper Peyton, the owner of the establishment, hadn't fired him for pouring icy-cold water on that jerk's lap.

He trudged across the Tybee Island sand, the crashing waves all around him. The flapping winds and birds spun above him—

And he had an idea for a new piece of work.

He would call it *The Mourning*.

His eyes were on the sand, looking for something. Something to start this new mixed-media design forming in his mind. He saw pieces of shredded driftwood, broken shells—

There.

A piece of sea glass.

He picked it up.

It was polished down to about two inches by three inches.

He held it up to the sun. Pinkish, purplish, periwinkle hues of translucence appeared before his eyes.

Whoa.

A gift from God.

He stared at it. And stared.

"What's that?"

Startled at the sweet voice that caressed his soul, Leon lost hold of the sea glass.

~

Sophie stood in the sand, shoeless, watching Leon pick up the sea glass he had dropped. He hadn't said a word to her, hadn't even acknowledged she was standing there.

Perhaps she should rephrase her question.

Perhaps he hadn't heard her.

She tried again. "Hey."

With a heave, he looked up. Barely.

His eyes were red.

Sophie's first thought was that he had sand in his eyes. That could do a number on his cornea. Yet as soon as she thought it, she knew that wasn't it.

She had arrived fifteen minutes ago, standing at a distance, watching him.

"What did you drop into the ocean?" Sophie asked softly.

Leon blew sand off the multihued sea glass. "A flower for Mom."

"Oh." Sophie couldn't hold it in, for some reason. She began to weep softly. She didn't know why.

"It's okay. Mom's with God now." Leon began to wipe off her tears with his fingers, smearing sand on her cheeks.

"Oops! Sorry!" He tried to brush it off.

Now sand was all over Sophie's face.

He started to laugh.

"I didn't order a skin peel." Sophie frowned, wiping off the sand with the edges of her three-quarter-length silk sleeves.

"You didn't order this either."

Leon touched her chin lightly, lifted it up, and brushed his thumb over her lower lip, ever so gently and hesitantly that it threw Sophie off balance.

She started to sink into the sand.

Or were her knees buckling?

She couldn't be sure.

All she knew was that she wanted more.

Leon dropped his thumb from her chin. "I'd better get going. Don't want to lose my job serving tables."

"Before you go, what was that about?"

Leon didn't reply.

"You don't know," Sophie suggested.

"Maybe I wanted..." He sighed. He was about to walk past Sophie, when he stopped to say, "What brings you here to Tybee?"

Sophie could not tell him her entire reason for being there, how the story about Leon's mom's drowning had touched her so much that she had felt drawn to this beach, to her memories of her own mom. Her older brother, Adam, had told her about how their parents had taken him—before Sophie had been born—to weekend picnics on these beaches near the Tybee Island Light Station.

She didn't know the area too well, and neither did she recall the exact picnic spot, but she knew where Leon lived, and she knew she could walk around his house to the beach to see what she might have missed out on.

A missing childhood.

As if by coming here, she could perhaps say her own goodbye to her own mother, whom she had never seen in her entire life. She had given birth to

Sophie in Savannah and then passed away a week later, leaving her and Adam in the care of a difficult father.

Yes, I said it.

Dad was difficult to live with.

It had to be by the mercy of God that his marriage to Xian had lasted this long. But Xian hadn't been there the first seven or eight years of Sophie's life after Mom's maternal death.

"Yes?" Leon asked.

"What?"

"What brings you here to Tybee?"

"I was only taking a drive to clear my head, and here I am."

"So Baxter didn't drive you this time?"

"I was on my way to work."

"A long circuitous route—and you're late for work, besides. Aren't you supposed to be there at nine o'clock or something?"

"How do you know my schedule?" Sophie followed him back to his house.

"I don't." Leon walked alongside Sophie. "Baxter starts work at nine, so I just assumed."

"You were right, but Dad's watching the gallery —remotely. He said I could come in later. I have several hours to kill. I was thinking of having lunch at Piper's."

"It's that way, ma'am. Half an hour." Leon

pointed between two houses. "Besides, don't you have some technical writing job to do until then?"

"I am starting a three-month sabbatical to take care of Dad and the gallery, and to get Jarvis off my back."

"Ah. If he ever touches you again, let me know."

"And?"

"I'll turn him into a mixed-media piece of some sort." Leon seemed serious about his commitment. He looked serious. Or at least tried to.

"So you're my self-appointed bodyguard now?" Sophie chuckled.

"Hang out with me, and he won't be a problem." He jangled his car keys. He didn't go inside the house.

Sophie figured he had apparently planned to leave or had been on his way out, when he went to the ocean to put a flower there for his...

Mom.

Tears pooled in her eyes.

Mom.

Leon stopped walking. His keys stilled in his palm. "Sophie?"

Sophie couldn't speak.

Leon put an arm around Sophie's shoulders.

Suddenly, Sophie realized how vulnerable she had made herself. She had just met this guy recently. Sure, Dad had known him for years, but that wasn't her story.

Somehow, minutes ago, Leon had put his thumb on her lips.

And what about all those unexpected hand-holdings since day one, as if they had known each other for a long time?

She'd have to find out if Dad had been talking to Leon about her life to the point that Leon was comfortable with her around.

Then again, maybe that had been his own personality of being at ease with everyone.

A really nice guy!

Whom she had kicked out of an opportunity of a career to display his artwork in her gallery—

Dad's gallery.

It's not my gallery.

He might have believed that she had come here to see him.

Truly, she hadn't.

Or...? What had been in her subconscious thoughts?

Mom.

My own mom.

"Ever since Saturday, when you told me about your mom, I've been thinking of mine," Sophie said.

"Oh. I didn't mean to cause..."

"Not your fault." Sophie waved at the big sky

and sea. "I didn't have the childhood that Adam—my brother—had, so I wanted to see..."

"See what you missed?"

Sophie nodded. Might as well admit it.

"One of these days, come early, and we'll watch the sunrise together," Leon said. "I'm free every morning until ten o'clock, except Sunday, when I'll be at church."

"Tomorrow morning?" Sophie felt anxious. "Tuesday?"

Perhaps, finally, she would be able to close this chapter of her life. This long chapter.

"Sounds good. Can you be here by six thirty? I'll make breakfast. We can eat on the beach. Sunrise will be around seven."

"How about you make coffee, and I'll bring bagels?" Sophie asked.

Leon rubbed his palms together. He seemed to respond well to the word *bagel*. "A date then."

A date?

Uh-oh.

CHAPTER ELEVEN

*L*eon was ready with the coffee and picnic blanket before he received a phone call from Sophie saying that she couldn't make it. Her dad had endured a bad night, and she had been up with him. She had a bad headache now. Xian had gone to the gallery this morning to fill in for Sophie. She'd take over after lunch.

"Baxter could've run the place," Sophie said. "But I sent him to Charleston to look at some paintings."

"Busy man."

"He's also talking to a gallery there about your exhibit."

"That's very kind." Of whom? Of Baxter? Sophie? Or was it Simon himself who had arranged that? Leon didn't want to ask any further.

"The least I can do. I'm sorry we can't display your...uh, artwork in our gallery. Dad's trying to get the next-door shop spaces ready, but there's a problem with mold... I'm sorry. I don't think the building will be ready for a while."

"No need to apologize. It's not your problem." Leon looked out to the ocean, wondering why he even bothered trying to display his artwork at all.

It's an acquired taste.

Those types of comments ricocheted in his brain. How many times had he heard that before?

Only art competition judges would appreciate your work.

"Leon?"

"I'm here." *I want to be miles away. Thousands of miles away.*

However, he knew he couldn't keep running.

"When I toured your studio on Saturday, did you show me everything you can do with art?" Sophie asked.

What kind of a question is that?

"Do I have more? Is that what you want to know?"

"In a way..."

"Don't worry about me, Miss Sophie. I'm going to be just fine. Worry about yourself." That came out wrong, but he couldn't retract it now. His frustration was on his sleeve, and it was waiting to explode.

"Worry about myself?" Sophie asked slowly. "What did you mean?"

"I can find another gallery on my own."

"I'm sure you can. Have a good day, Leon."

Click.

Leon buried his face in his hands. He wished he'd been more self-controlled in his speech and...

And actions.

He had freely held her hands—she hadn't stopped him—and he had nearly kissed her—she had welcomed it.

Now she had hung up on him.

What should I do now? Call her back? Apologize? What?

~

*I*f it was possible to be bothered by one thing for hours on end, this had to be it. Leon spent the rest of that Tuesday in a bad mood at Piper's Place. He restrained it somewhat when waiting tables, but once he got back into his car again after his shift had ended, the dark cloud still hovered over his head.

It remained there until the next morning when a

thundershower woke him up too early at four o'clock.

His mother's Bible in his hand, he shuffled out to the kitchen, made some coffee, and sat down at a folding table to gather his thoughts.

"Lord, I'm at my wit's end. I've always wanted to be an artist, a sculptor, and spend all my life just making art. But I'm waiting tables to make that dream come true."

He opened the Bible to where he had placed a bookmark. It was a memory verse from his Sunday School at Riverside Chapel. Matthew 5:23-24 waited for him to reread it.

Therefore if you bring your gift to the altar, and there remember that your brother has something against you, leave your gift there before the altar, and go your way. First be reconciled to your brother, and then come and offer your gift.

Leon cringed. His phone conversation with Sophie returned to his mind.

Do I have more? Is that what you want to know?

His own tone in his reply to Sophie began to hurt.

Worry about yourself.

Behind him, the coffeemaker called. He poured and drank the bitter cup.

Looked at the clock.
Only a quarter to five.
He prayed for wisdom. Insight. Discernment.
He reread Matthew 5:23.
First, I need to be reconciled to Sophie.
Then, I can come to worship God.

CHAPTER TWELVE

S ophie stared at the woven tapestry on the wall of Simon's Gallery. She stepped forward to take a closer look at a corner of the brand-new work. Recycled materials, yes, but turned into art. It was clearly a cut above what Leon Watts could produce.

"This is a great find, Baxter," she said.

Baxter beamed with happiness.

Sophie had never seen anyone so happy. Except for her perpetually happy puppy that she had when she had been a little child. The puppy that had always smiled, bright eyes and all, and wagged its tail whenever Sophie was around. Up to the day it was run over by the garbage truck.

Ever since then, Sophie had refused to own a pet.

Any pet.

"She has another series made of sea glass, driftwood, and whatever she could find outside her beach home."

Sea glass? It reminded Sophie of that piece of sea glass that Leon had held in his hand on Monday morning. She wondered if he was going to do something with that.

"How did you find this artist?" Sophie tried to remember her name. She hadn't always been interested in art, but Dad had filled her in on things, and she had accompanied him to art exhibitions across the world—when Dad had been up to traveling. That was before his health worsened and he had hired Baxter to do the acquisitions for him.

"I got her name from Leon," Baxter said.

"Leon Watts?"

"One and only. He knew this Cholandra from art school, he told me."

Cholandra with no last name.

Sophie wondered if there was more to it. Did they have a history together, for example?

Sophie found herself walking away from the tapestry, when she spotted someone walking in through the front door.

Leon. What does he want?

Turning away, Sophie made a quiet dash for her

office—but before she made it to the door, Leon's words reached her ear.

"May I speak with you, Miss Sophie?" It was a calm voice but with a sense of urgency.

"I'm busy this morning."

"Just two minutes of your time."

"It's never just two minutes, don't you realize? Often it's more like five."

"Five then. Five minutes of your time, please?"

Leon's pleading face gnawed at Sophie's heart.

She stood there. "What is it?"

"May we talk somewhere private?"

"About?"

"About my poor choice of words on the phone yesterday."

"I've already forgotten," Sophie found herself saying.

"No, you haven't." A smile escaped Leon's lips.

"What makes you say that?"

"I can see it in your eyes." Leon leaned closer and lowered his voice. "You want to know what I meant by, 'Worry about yourself.' Am I right?"

"No, I don't." *Yes, I do.* "I don't care." *Oh yes, I care.*

"Just two—five minutes. Then I'll leave and you'll never see me again."

Somehow Sophie's heart ached. She led him to Dad's office. Kept the door opened.

Twenty minutes later, Leon was still talking, sitting in the art deco chair across from Dad's old table, trying to explain why he had told Sophie to worry about herself.

He fumbled all over the place.

Finally, Sophie put her palm up. "In summary, you're saying I'm no better off than you."

Leon's jaw dropped. "Exactly."

"So why don't you just come right out and say it?"

"I was expressing myself."

"Sure."

"I'm no wordsmith," Leon said.

"That, you're not."

"Now that we're transparent with each other, will you have a picnic with me?"

Sophie hesitated. Then she asked him point blank, "What would be the purpose of it?"

"I'll sketch. Show you I can do more than just mixed media."

"You can do that any time."

"I want you to see me do it."

"To prove a point?" Sophie almost laughed. "Have some confidence in yourself. You don't need to prove anything to me."

"I want to."

But why? Sophie couldn't put a finger on his

pulse. "Regardless, your mixed-media exhibition is not showing at Simon's Gallery."

Blunt.

"I understand," Leon said. "It's important for you to know that I'm an artist."

"If you are, God already knows."

Silence.

Sophie waited.

He didn't say any more.

"All right. What are you going to sketch?"

"Paint. Sketch and paint."

"All right. What are you going to paint?"

"You."

"Me?" Sophie was startled. "What for?"

"Did you know that your face has perfect symmetry?" Leon asked.

"Ah, the braces paid off."

Leon laughed.

Silence.

Something was happening. Sophie wasn't sure what. If he wanted to paint her portrait, should she stop him? After all, it was obvious he needed some self-confidence.

Dad had said that Leon was talented.

Then go be talented somewhere else—

No.

I want to see this.

"Sheryl out front should have some canvas. How about oil pastel?"

Leon's eyebrows rose. "A challenge?"

"Why not? And right now."

"The lighting in this office is terrible."

"An excuse?"

"No, no. But I only have an hour to get to Piper's Place."

"So start now." Sophie waited for Leon to think about it.

"How about we start tomorrow? I'll bring my own canvas and pastels."

Sophie didn't want to guess what Leon was up to, but she had to know. "Nothing weird, right?"

"Let me surprise you."

"What are you saying?"

"Nothing. So how about I come here at nine every morning and you sit for me for half an hour?"

"I start work at nine. You'll have to come at eight thirty."

"Fair enough," Leon said. "When it's done, it's yours if you want it."

Do I want it? Could I want it?

Sophie had checked his portfolio. No portraits.

Could he paint her at all?

She had doubts.

CHAPTER THIRTEEN

$\mathcal{T}$he next morning, bright and early—well, at eight thirty—Leon Watts stood outside Simon's Gallery, texting Baxter to open the door for him.

He couldn't wait to get started. He paced the sidewalk, getting a bit antsy from too much coffee. His old and worn bag hanging off a shoulder, and a roll of canvas under the arm, he couldn't stop walking back and forth, until he spotted someone coming to the door.

On the drive here from Tybee Island, Leon had figured out forty or fifty different colors he could use on the portrait.

Yet when he saw who unlocked the door for him, he forgot everything he had rehearsed in his head in the car.

"Good morning." Sophie pulled the door back to let him in.

"Good morning. I texted Baxter." Oddly, he felt a spurt of jealousy. Now where did that come from? *Well, how did Sophie get Baxter's text?*

"He's in the back. We were taking inventory. I told him to keep at it. I can get the door. Come on in."

See? No need to worry about it.

"I'm thinking too much," Leon blurted.

"Pardon me?"

"Nothing. Lead the way."

Sophie stopped. "That's what I was going to ask you. Where should we go?"

"Where can we go?"

"We could sit in the middle of the gallery. But I don't want to turn this into a sidewalk artist thingy."

"Excuse me?" Leon felt offended.

"That came out all wrong." Sophie closed her eyes. Took a deep breath.

Leon waited.

"I meant that we don't have the biggest gallery space here. Dad's still working on the building next door, and frankly, I think he should just forget it. The monthly payment would double, and there's no guarantee of income... I spoke too much."

A smile hung on Leon's face. "We're not having a good start, are we?"

"I need some air."

"Me too. How about outdoors? It's pretty nice outside at this time in the morning."

"The roof then."

"The roof?" Leon liked the idea. "Creative thought."

"Is that a compliment or an insult?" Sophie didn't look like she was trying to argue with him.

"I meant it literally," Leon explained.

"Okay. Just wanted to know. I'm tired of people playing guessing games. I can't read between the lines. I prefer words spoken to be in black and white."

"I promise that I will always speak my mind with you."

Yikes. What did I just promise?

~

*B*etween Baxter and Leon, they hauled up a bright magenta armchair and plopped it right in the middle of the rooftop patio overlooking River Street, the Rousakis Riverfront Plaza, and Hutchinson Island across the Savannah River. The morning hour was cool this October, a slight breeze completing the outdoor studio.

As Sophie took her seat in the plush armchair, she saw her cream-and-black dress pants pop against the almost-fluorescent color of the armchair upholstery. Without asking for permission from the artist, she started checking her email on her iPhone.

Every now and then, Sophie eyed Leon as he set up his canvas on the easel he had borrowed from Baxter. His barstool was visible on the other side of the easel, but she could not see what he had on the canvas.

He sharpened his pencil to make an outline on the canvas. "I didn't know you have a rooftop garden."

"I rarely come up here. Xian waters the flowers. Dad said they sometimes eat lunch up here."

"Today would be a good day to eat lunch here. The weather forecast says it's going to be in the seventies, no more."

Sophie didn't look up. She frowned at the incessant emails from Jarvis. She didn't have to read them. He wanted another date.

Persistence was one thing, but this was bordering on harassment.

"Everything okay?"

Sophie straightened her back. "You remember my bad date night?"

"Only last Friday."

"He's been sending me emails, text messages, literally every single day."

"Block him. Report as spam." Leon started to sketch.

"I'm doing that now. I didn't before because I thought...maybe it was related to work. I need more income."

"But his company is a bridge you can totally burn. No reason to work with someone like that."

"I don't want trouble." Sophie started to think that perhaps she should dig up her résumé, and send it out to other businesses in the country, who might need a freelance technical writer. After Dad returned to work, this short-term income would dry up. Her last contracts had all been with Jarvis's company.

At the back of her mind, she wondered what else she could do other than technical writing.

This job was getting old. She worked alone most of the time.

Dad and Xian had both said she needed to get out and mingle.

Mingle with people? She'd rather sit in front of her computer and write another manual or user guide, thank you very much.

"Trouble?" Leon leaned his head to one side. The rest of his torso—and that plaid shirt again— was hidden behind the canvas.

He was wearing a pair of ripped jeans and comfortable-looking flip-flops.

Sophie tried not to meet his gaze.

Funny how she found it easy to talk with Leon, like they had known each other for a while, like they were meant to know each other.

She kept her eyes on her iPhone, which was now displaying text messages from her stepmother, complaining yet again about Dad. Yeah, she'd have to agree with Xian. Dad was a poor patient.

Quietly, she prayed for God to quickly heal Dad so he could go back to work and get out of Xian's hair.

"I know trouble," Leon continued, not being privy to Sophie's thoughts. "I know trouble on every side, but I remind myself that God has overcome the world. John 16:33."

Sophie looked it up on her Bible app. She read it aloud. "John 16:33 says, 'These things I have spoken to you, that in Me you may have peace. In the world you will have tribulation; but be of good cheer, I have overcome the world.' There you go."

Read aloud, the refreshing passage of Scripture filled the rooftop patio.

Slowly, Leon spoke. "You have a pretty reading voice."

"I thought we were focusing on God's Word."

"Yes, ma'am." Leon went back to work.

CHAPTER FOURTEEN

"*T*hat's too bad, Leon." Cholandra's face moved in and out of the screen on Leon's phone.

Leon realized he probably shouldn't have unloaded his woes on his ex-girlfriend, but they had remained friends these several years, and she had called him this morning at this time in his life, in the middle of his financial crisis—which was pretty much on his mind.

"Why don't you call her dad and remind him that he agreed to display your work?" Cholandra asked. "She didn't sign the contract with you. He did."

"I don't want to cause a problem in the family."

"You have no money for food and rent. I say they've already caused a problem for you."

"I'll find another gallery."

"Better do it quickly, Leon. They don't pay right away, as you know."

"If you have any leads, I'm all ears."

Silence.

"Cholandra?" Leon wondered what the problem was. All he did was ask for suggestions.

"You could tour with me," Cholandra said slowly.

"Tour?"

"I'm taking some of my works across North America. I'm scheduled to be in Toronto on Thursday. Join me?"

Now it was Leon's turn to be silent. He wasn't going back to that life with her.

That life?

It had begun with art, but it had not ended that way.

In spite of his mom's issues, she had advised him to stay strong in the Lord and not be bought by sweet talk.

Cholandra had never been one to sweet talk, but she had been strongly manipulative.

No more.

"I don't know..." Leon cringed at his own words.

"That's not an absolute no, is it?" Cholandra chuckled. "Think about it, and let me know tonight. I leave tomorrow."

"Tomorrow is Sunday. I'm at church."

Cholandra seemed to ignore that big part of Leon's life. "We can drive together."

Drive together?

Leon had moved on, hadn't he? Why was Cholandra suggesting another collaboration?

"Is this why you called?" Leon asked.

"I hate traveling alone."

"Is there no one else?"

"There is no one else."

At this time. Knowing her, she'd have a new boyfriend before her art tour was over. "I can't go. I have a day job now."

Cholandra laughed. "And what might that be?"

"It's a decent job, so don't mock me."

"I'm not mocking you. You could be rich if you come with me."

I doubt it. "Life on the road is not for me."

"You're the one talking, Leon. Didn't you just travel the world for almost two years?"

"Eighteen months." Leon glanced at the clock and started walking toward his bathroom. "I have to go, Cholandra. Have to get to work."

"About Toronto?"

"I'll get back to you."

"You have a new girlfriend? Is that why you won't go with me to Toronto?"

"No. I can't haul my large displays all over the

continent without preparation. You leave tomorrow."

"If you had time, you would've come with me?" Cholandra's voice brightened.

"I'll pray about it."

"Don't play the God card with me, Leon. You didn't have a problem three years ago."

"That was then."

"And what is now?"

Good question. What is now?

～

*L*eon remembered Sophie's face, as though she were standing right in front of him right now. He closed his eyes to remember her rare smile.

They were standing on the beach.

He was holding the piece of sea glass in his hand.

It was morning.

He had just said goodbye to Mom.

And then Sophie was there, opening a new chapter in his life.

When he opened his eyes, Leon found himself standing alone in the middle of his studio, two pieces of broken oil pastels in his palm and an unfinished portrait in front of him.

Colors.

I need more colors.

If this were a watercolor painting, he would splash the colors haphazardly.

But this was to be a work of symmetry.

Somewhere at the back of his mind, he wanted to glue something three-dimensional to it. *Yes, truly.*

His art teacher back in college had said that Leon gravitated toward mixed media.

This painting was only to prove to Sophie that he wasn't one dimensional. He was a well-rounded artist, though his preference was singularly mixed media.

Could Sophie blame him?

Why would he need to change anything for her?

As he blended yellow ochre with white pastels, Leon felt even worse.

What about God?

Have I changed anything in my life to please God?

CHAPTER FIFTEEN

The noonday sun shone through Dad's summer kitchen, casting light and shadows on the old kitchen table, light that played with the blue water goblet that Sophie held in her hands.

It had been a pleasant Saturday morning for Sophie. She had gotten up early after a restful night's sleep, puttered around, and then headed here for lunch with Dad and Xian.

Truth be told, she hadn't had a good night's sleep in ages.

What had changed?

She wasn't sure. It couldn't have been the gallery. Then again, the gallery had brought out her artistic side, long suppressed. Well, she had been busy working, hadn't she? One couldn't blame her for putting aside hobbies in the name of work.

In the name of work?

What about doing something in the Name of the Lord instead?

Sophie breathed in deeply.

Yes. I want to do that. But someday.

Right now, there were bills to pay. That was why she had taken that job as a technical writer. Freelancing had enabled her to live debt-free. However, it wasn't something she'd want to do the rest of her life.

What would it feel like to do something you truly like but might not pay much?

Like what Leon was doing?

Leon Watts.

A thorn in Sophie's side.

Lunches with Dad and Xian had been getting more interesting since the day Sophie had told Leon to take his artwork back to where it came from.

"That's unfair," Dad said as he speared the olives in his salad.

Xian returned from their summer kitchen with a basket of fresh rolls. "What's unfair?"

Dad pointed to Sophie.

Sophie didn't say a word.

"At least pay him," Dad said.

"Pay who for what?" Xian sat down.

Dad turned to Xian. "Talk some sense into my daughter, will you?"

They waited.

Sophie didn't know what to say. Really. Truly.

"Go on?" Xian offered her a roll.

Sophie took it. She didn't need all those carbohydrates, but there was no reason to add more strife to her already awkward situation.

"Leon offered to paint a portrait of me." Sophie buttered the roll. "He wants to prove that he can do more than glue recycled junkyard finds together."

"See there?" Dad snapped. "Now you're rude too."

Xian hushed him.

Their eyes were on Sophie.

Waiting.

Sophie put down her butter knife on her plate.

Usually she'd rather not talk to her parents about such things. Matters of the heart, confusion in her mind. Stuff like that.

"If I didn't agree to manage your gallery for a couple of months, none of this would've happened," Sophie said. "I would be safe in my cubicle, minding my own business."

"Ah, so we expanded your world," Dad concluded.

Sophie had always been transparent with Dad,

and there was no reason not to be now. "Or you've confused it further."

"The last time you were confused about anything was when you were madly in love with that quarterback in high school," Dad said.

"Have you met someone?" Xian asked.

Have I?

"Sometimes when you have matters of the heart like that, it can cause your decisions to not make sense," Xian said.

"Really?" Dad rubbed his chin. "Maybe you're on to something, Xian."

He turned to Sophie. "For instance, why in the world would Leon offer to paint your portrait?"

"Because he wants me to put his mixed media on display in the gallery." It was all Sophie could think of.

"And?"

"There's nothing else. He needs the money. He wants validation as an artist."

"He's not new to the scene," Dad said. "I displayed his artwork two years ago before his mother passed away."

"Did you sell them?"

"Some. Wasn't a lot."

"See there?" Sophie's lips quivered. "So maybe I felt sorry for him. Maybe I want to help."

"It's my gallery, but you know me," Dad said. "I

asked you to run it for three months, and I respect your business decisions. But if we can get that next-door building cleaned up, I'd display his work there."

"That's not going to happen anytime soon," Xian said.

"Oh?" Sophie asked.

"Mold."

"That." Dad grunted. "And I'm losing money dealing with that."

"Yikes." Sophie wondered why it had just been one thing after another for her parents. "See there, Dad? You need to display artwork that brings in money. Your gallery is not thriving at this time."

Sophie leaned back. "Truth be told, I'm the wrong person for this. Dad, I'm a technical writer, not an art gallery director."

"You have a business mind," Dad said. "And remember all our trips to art galleries around the country?"

"That was fun."

"I'd rather trust you to hold up the fort than anyone else."

"What about Baxter? He's a very good manager." Sophie was confident that her assessment was right.

"He's not family."

"On the other hand, family members may not

always be the best hires or business partners," Xian added.

"See?" Sophie pointed to Xian. "Wise words indeed."

Xian's hand reached out toward Sophie. "When your dad is all better, the gallery will be off your hands."

"Thank you." *And when will that be?*

"You'll do fine." Xian patted Sophie's arm. "Now, tell me. You like Leon?"

CHAPTER SIXTEEN

*S*he's *wearing burlap again.*

Leon had anticipated that as he watched Sophie close the stairwell door and cross the rooftop patio toward the armchair—which he had brought up on the elevator near the stairwell using a cart he borrowed from Baxter.

On the armrest, Leon had placed the sea glass he had picked up on the beach a week ago.

He wasn't going to say anything. He wanted to see if Sophie noticed color at all.

Sophie sat down without seeing it. "What? Why are you looking at me like that?"

Leon shrugged.

"Did I forget to wish you a good morning?"

"You said that when you opened the door just now."

"I did?"

"You're starting to forget things?" Leon asked.

She looked nervous this Monday morning. Why?

"I hope you didn't think I made you pose for your portrait," Leon said.

"You suggested it. I agreed to it."

So let's get on with it? "I wanted you to know that I finished the portrait at home."

Sophie's jaw dropped. "Already?"

"Told you that your face is symmetrical. I remember symmetrical faces."

"You mean you only had to memorize half of it?"

Leon chuckled. "Want to see it?"

"I don't know..."

Leon pointed to the covered painting.

"So why set all this up?" Sophie waved her hands.

"I want you to remember the moment."

"What moment?"

Leon stepped toward Sophie. "This setting. This outdoor studio. The garden around us. The sky above us."

"So take a picture."

"Good idea." Leon dug for his phone. He couldn't find it. "I must've left it in the car."

"Use mine." Sophie swiped her iPhone.

They took an unplanned selfie.

It was the last thing Leon had expected to do with Sophie.

And she hadn't even seen the painting.

Neither had she noticed the sea glass.

~

*S*hocked was the word that Sophie had been looking for, but what ricocheted in her mind was another word.

Horrified.

Stunned, she was unable to speak as she stood there staring at the portrait of her that Leon had painted. He had used up at least two boxes of his pastel crayons or whatever they were called.

And all he could come up with was this?

The square canvas, three feet by three, was covered with streaks of neon colors from corner to corner, and side to side. A bazillion colors of all shades and tones. Sophie had never seen any artist who could combine such a huge collection of colors on such a small canvas.

The only colors not found on there were pure black and pure white. Why?

She couldn't breathe.

Leon stood there, staring at her staring at the painting.

"Well?" he finally said.

Before Sophie could respond, Luke 6:41 came to her mind.

And why do you look at the speck in your brother's eye, but do not perceive the plank in your own eye?

Sophie held her tongue and began to pray.

Lord, his speck is very big. He just ruined my symmetry.

"Well?" Leon tried again.

Sophie tried to find something nice to say about the painting. "Colors."

"That's the idea."

"How many colors are there?"

"Two hundred and twenty-one bold and beautiful colors."

"No kidding." Sophie shivered in the autumn breeze. "What are you calling this piece?"

"*Sophie 221.*"

"My name?"

"Well, plus two hundred and twenty-one colors."

"Seriously?"

"It's how I see you."

"Me? This is how you see me?"

"It's not you, per se, but a representation of you." His voice was strained. "You don't like it."

Sophie stared at a few golden strands of something floating in the middle of the canvas. "What are those?"

"Your hair."

"What?"

"A few strands of your hair."

Sophie leaned closer. "You mean they're stuck to the oil pastels?"

"No. I painted it in."

Sophie stepped closer to the painting. "Oh. Very realistic. They have shadows and all."

"Thank you."

"What about the rest of my face?" *All that talk about symmetry?*

"It's hidden."

"I can see that. Like you painted over my face."

Leon stepped between Sophie and his painting, as if to protect his masterpieces—as if she might be thinking of something violent.

Me? Violent?

Sophie placed her palm on her chest. She thought her heart was pulsating wildly.

"Shall we show it to your dad?" Leon asked.

"I—uh... I'll send him a picture." Sophie couldn't believe how her hands trembled as she swiped her iPhone.

It was a miracle that her phone was still in her

hand, actually. She could barely hold the phone still.

All those colors!

They sent sparks into her head.

"May I?" Leon opened his palm.

Sophie handed him her phone.

A few snaps away, and Sophie was ready to send it to Dad.

She wondered what he would say.

"You hate my work," Leon concluded.

An understatement.

It seemed to Sophie that this artist overdid everything, from laundry to pots and pans, and now pastels.

Some might say it meant he was showing passion.

Passion?

Sophie stared at Leon. Apparently he had more to say.

"I guess this is the wrong time to ask you something," he said.

"Like what?" Sophie snapped.

"Like watching the sunrise from the beach with me this Saturday morning?" Leon asked. "It's not going to rain. I checked."

"Are you kidding me?" And on that note, Sophie walked off.

"I guess that's a no," Leon's voice echoed behind her as she slammed the door to the stairwell leading down to the gallery.

CHAPTER SEVENTEEN

*L*eon sat alone on his beach blanket, watching the sun rise into the sky.

Around him was the usual crowd of neighbors, early risers all, walking their dogs, walking with coffee mugs in hand, walking with their significant others...

He reread the text message.

Can't make it. Sorry.

When Sophie had come to her senses on Thursday, Leon had asked her again about the breakfast picnic.

She had said yes.

However, this morning, thirty minutes before their picnic, she had texted to cancel.

On that note, Leon knew that she hated the painting.

Leon felt conflicted. Sure, he wanted his artwork displayed in Simon's Gallery, but he'd rather have Sophie's friendship. Something had started between them.

Nevertheless, as his bills accumulated, Leon knew he had to make a living, Sophie notwithstanding.

Cholandra's offer of a continental art tour seemed more and more enticing to Leon.

Art Awareness Tour.

He googled the event and found out that there were twenty artists involved in the year-round project. He emailed Cholandra to find out what the returns looked like.

Unfortunately, Cholandra had no idea. All she could tell Leon was that she was raking up her credit cards with traveling expenses. Local galleries would host the exhibition, but she had to pay for gas to lug all her artworks from city to city and set them up.

Wouldn't the visibility and discoverability make up for the lack of immediate income?

No.

He had to pay his bills. Now.

Then Leon found out that he could make as few stops as he wanted. Practically, he could display his artwork in just a few cities. He didn't have to stay for the entire tour.

That could be an option.

He wanted to run it by someone, to ask for a second opinion. The only person he could think of was Simon himself. Would he be available to talk?

Even though it was now seven o'clock in the morning, it was too early for Leon to call an elderly gentleman recovering from a broken leg.

What about God?

Leon stretched out his legs on the picnic blanket. He looked far away into the distant horizon, where the ocean had taken Mom to depths unknown.

Why did You allow her to do that, Lord?

It seemed easy to blame God, and he had done it so many times.

But now, sitting here on the picnic blanket alone, he had no one to talk to but God.

The chicken biscuits in the paper sack next to him had probably gone cold. He had gotten up early to get to Island Breakfast to Go to get them.

How on earth had he even thought that Sophie would agree to have breakfast with him on the beach? What sort of an invitation was that?

It had been daring.

Or stupid.

Lord Jesus, I am wandering around aimlessly. Please give me direction.

Leon leaned back on the blanket, arms behind

his head, eyes closed again, feeling the warming sun on his face. It must be getting cloudy, because he felt a shadow covering the sun.

"Another puffy cloud..."

He opened his eyes to take a peek.

"I'm not a puffy cloud," she said.

~

"I thought you weren't coming." Leon sat straight up on the picnic blanket.

The brown color of the faded blanket somehow matched the faded plaid shirt he was wearing.

How can a man have so many plaid shirts? And look good in every single one of them?

Standing there at the edge of his picnic blanket, Sophie waited for the invitation to sit down. Leon seemed to be surprised that she was even here at all.

"I felt bad when I saw your text. I didn't expect you to stand in line for half an hour to get me a chicken biscuit," Sophie said. "If I'd known, I would have canceled sooner to save you the trouble."

"No trouble. I could eat your biscuit for lunch."

"Well, sorry to spoil your lunch. I'm here now. May I sit down?"

Leon's face reddened. "Sorry. Please do."

Sophie kicked off her sandals and sat at an edge of the blanket.

Leon handed her a chicken biscuit.

"Do you think it's still good?" Sophie asked.

"As in, will the fall weather temperature put germs into the chicken?"

Sophie nodded.

"Well, it has been about fifty minutes since I got back from the breakfast place."

"So if we eat quickly, we'll be fine?"

"Their paper wrappers are insulated." Leon showed her.

"If we both fall sick and don't make it to church tomorrow, it's your fault." Sophie laughed.

"I'll say grace." Leon bowed his head to ask God to bless the food and not let them get sick from the lukewarm chicken biscuit.

Taking a bite, Sophie declared it to be delicious.

"It's a new breakfast place. I wanted to get a job there, but there are no openings."

"No wonder."

"I'm going to keep trying."

People watching kept them occupied for a while.

"I'm glad you came." Leon wadded up his chicken biscuit wrapper.

Sophie could not read his mind. "I'm sorry I wasn't sure how to respond."

"I put you in an awkward position. I wanted you to come."

"Because?"

"I don't really know why. I feel..."

Sophie waited.

"I feel drawn to you somehow."

Sophie prayed for the right words to say. She was at some sort of crossroads now. She had accepted his invitation for a picnic for two. This could end either badly or happily for both of them.

"I wanted to come, but I was afraid." *There, I said it.*

"Afraid of me?" Leon poured coffee for both of them.

Sophie noticed that Leon kept the mug with the chipped lip for himself and gave her what looked like a newer mug.

"I'm more afraid of your art," Sophie said.

"Well, I'm glad you're not afraid of me."

There was nothing else for them to talk about. Breakfast was over, the sun was warming up, and Sophie wanted to leave.

But why?

She had come all the way from downtown Savannah only to leave?

She hadn't been here but twenty or thirty minutes. In that span of time they hadn't spoken more than several sentences to each other.

Sophie noticed that Leon had made no attempt to hold her hand.

He had so easily held her hand the first day they had met, when he wanted to show her the cot in the back room. However, Sophie chalked that up to his lack of awareness, or perhaps to his natural ease around people.

Maybe it's an artist thing.

"I've been meaning to ask you something," Leon said. "Since you're here, perhaps you can tell me why you dislike my painting so much."

"Dislike? I detest it."

"Because?"

"I don't have to explain anything." Sophie remained seated, but she felt like leaving now.

"I want to know." He reached for her. "It's not that bad, is it?"

CHAPTER EIGHTEEN

*I*t seemed too painful for Sophie to speak
of it, to explain why she didn't care for
his artwork, and Leon wished he had never asked.

And yet once he had asked her, Sophie looked
ready—almost relieved—that she could tell her story.

"My dad raised my brother and me by
himself," Sophie said. "Adam would regale me
with stories of his childhood that I had never experienced myself."

She looked away.

The morning breeze blew about her wavy ash-
blond hair. Sunny highlights aside, her hair looked
like the color of ginger ale, which Leon remembered
using on that oil pastel painting.

He wondered what Simon's Gallery was going
to do with it. One way or another, he was splitting

the profits with the gallery, and that was how it went.

If he had left it to Sophie, Leon was sure she would stash it in a closet somewhere.

But that was a battle for another day.

He was supposed to be listening to Sophie, who hadn't spoken since she mentioned her brother.

"I wish I was old enough to have known my mom." Sophie looked away.

"Life is hard sometimes."

Sophie turned pensive again.

Leon offered her more coffee, but she declined.

"The Bible does say we're to honor our parents," Leon said. "It's hard to do that when they have issues."

"I'm sure each of us has issues. It's part of our sin nature, isn't it?"

Leon felt his heart warm up. Only a true believer would speak like that.

"Thanks be to God for saving our souls through Jesus Christ," he said.

"Amen."

"If not for Him, I don't know where I'd be," Leon added.

"Me too. You know, sometimes I wonder why my mom did not believe in Jesus."

"How do you know she didn't?"

"Dad told me." Sophie brushed a wayward

strand of hair from her eyes. "He also told me that Mom was an artist. She loved bright colors."

An artist in the Kowalski family.

Leon hadn't expected that.

"Is that why you only wear plain clothes? You didn't want to remember your colorful mom?"

Leon didn't know how that question rolled off his tongue.

There she was, sitting there in yet another shade of burlap, and he had to say such a thing. It could very well mark the end of their wonderful morning conversation.

"Plain?" Sophie asked.

Might as well go all the way to the end zone. "Yes, dull and uninspiring colors of black and white and burlap. Like mourning clothes."

Sophie bristled. "I wear charcoal too."

"The color of ash."

Sophie stared at him. Then she broke into a quick laugh. It sounded like a jab. A counterpunch. "Don't read too much into what I wear."

"I'm an artist. I'm all about symbolism."

"Yeah?"

"Yeah."

"Then explain to me why you spent six—or seven—days painting streaks of colors on canvas and call it a portrait."

"I wish you a colorful life."

"Is that good or bad?"

Leon smiled. "I think it's good."

"Only if it comes from God, I think."

"I like the way you think."

"We're repeating words." Sophie crossed her legs away from Leon. She looked up into the sky. "I'll have to leave shortly. I need to go check on Dad."

"How's he doing?"

"A difficult patient."

"I'm gathering Xian is patient."

"To an extent. Eventually, she might snap. Dad can be awfully needy when he's down."

"Just several more weeks." Leon prayed for courage before he said the next thing. "Would you like to take a walk?"

Sophie hesitated. Then: "Sure."

Leon was on his feet before she was. He reached for her hands. "I think you like me."

"It's your plaid shirts." Sophie placed her hand on his chest.

"Is that right?" He felt the warmth of her palm through his shirt.

Leon pulled her toward him. He planted a gentle kiss on her soft cheek.

So soft.

Leon wondered what her lips felt like...

His lips melded into hers. She tasted like coffee, biscuit, and...

"Chocolate." Leon pulled away. "You brought me chocolate?"

Sophie cringed. "Well..."

"You left it in your car?"

"I...uh...sort of...ate it on the way here."

"You ate some. That's totally okay by me."

"I ate it all."

"You ate it all?" Leon wasn't sure what to think.

"Technically, I haven't given it to you."

"Because you ate it before you got here," Leon teased. "So much for self-control."

Sophie ribbed him. "What about that kiss? You didn't have any self-control either."

"Sure I did. I was very controlled." Leon thumbed the base of her jawline. "I saved more kisses for later."

"Oh."

CHAPTER NINETEEN

*R*esisting Dad had its consequences, one of which was his incessant texts and phone calls and threats related to birthdays and Christmas. Truly, Sophie couldn't care less, but this was Dad. She couldn't ignore him.

By Monday, Dad wasn't talking to Sophie. All because of that painting.

By Tuesday, Sophie had given up trying to dissuade Dad from hanging *Sophie 221* on the gallery wall.

He wanted it near the front door.

With her picture next to it.

For comparison.

Aarrgghh...

Sophie didn't want to see Leon's oil pastel painting of her, so she had dispatched Baxter to do the dirty deed. She only found out later that Baxter had tweeted a photo of it to the art world, and as common and profound as the bizarre portrait was, Baxter had inadvertently kicked off a sudden maelstrom of oil pastel trending hashtags.

By Thursday, bids had arrived en masse for the painting.

Sophie took the afternoon off to go shopping for a black dress and black pumps to go with it.

Nursing a headache, she shut off her phone and went alone to Piper's Place, hoping for some peace and quiet and a hot meal. Simon's Gallery closed at six o'clock, so all the hullabaloo should be over by now.

The entire time she read the menu, she forgot that Leon worked there.

And here he was.

"May I get you something to drink?" Leon said, rather enthusiastically.

"Oh, it's you."

"Oh, it's me." His shoulders sagged. "I'm sorry I've caused you and your dad to quarrel the last two days. I really did not mean for a painting to be so much trouble."

"Dad has ordered Baxter to hang it in the gallery by the front door, and that's the way it goes."

Leon pulled out his notepad to take her order. "But you still don't like the painting."

122

"You don't need my approval."

Sophie wasn't sure what had gotten into her. Everyone could tell that painting did not look like her at all, so why would she be upset about it?

Besides, what had this man done to her to cause her to react this way?

He had been kind to her. In fact, it was here a couple of weeks ago that he had rescued her from a bad date.

And then there was the kiss on the beach on Saturday morning.

Now Sophie felt horrible about her own attitude.

But she wasn't going to apologize.

"If you must know, there are a few colors I didn't put into your portrait," Leon said quietly.

"Stop calling it my portrait. A few strands of hair do not a portrait make."

"That's a good one." Leon glanced behind him. "We'll have to talk another time. I'm going to get into trouble if I don't take your order. Other customers are waiting."

"Sorry. Water with lime, and..." Sophie scanned the menu and ordered the restaurant's signature southwestern tortilla soup. "That's all I want right now."

"All right. Thank you."

Before Leon returned, Sophie decided to turn on her phone.

She had missed an avalanche of messages and emails. Mostly from Dad and Xian and Baxter and Dad and...Adam?

What does my brother want?

She checked his text message, and nearly slid off her seat.

Why does Adam want me to call Dad? Why call him? Is he dying?

She tapped Dad's name to read his latest messages.

Oh. It's about that painting.

Again.

Sophie couldn't believe her brother was now involved. Who cared about a portrait that didn't look anything like her—save for a strand of hair?

Sophie had to keep reading, out of respect for Dad taking the time to text her. It looked like he had sent it half an hour ago.

Whoa. This cannot be real.

Leon came back with her glass of water, and he looked like he was just as oblivious as she had been to today's development.

Sophie wondered whether she should be the first to break the news to him.

It wouldn't be fair otherwise.

"Have you checked your messages lately?" Sophie asked as Leon handed her a straw.

"Nope. We can't use our phones until after work. Is there a problem?"

"That painting?"

"The one you hate so much?" Leon grinned. "That we just talked about minutes ago?"

Sophie nodded. "I don't have to worry about it anymore."

"Oh no. Don't tell me it's in storage."

"No. It's being shipped out."

"Someone bought it?" His eyes—bluer than blue —widened.

"Guess how much?"

"I just want to break even."

"And more. A collector bought it two hours ago for seven thousand dollars."

"Thousand?" Leon leaned against the table. "You're kidding me."

"Do I look like I'm kidding?" Sophie waited for Leon to regain his composure.

"If I sold ten of those..."

"Leon." Sophie stopped him. "That's an unusual case. The next one might not sell for that much. From Baxter's research, he thinks two or three thousand dollars are more likely."

"Okay. So I'll just have to paint more."

"I guess."

"Thank you," Leon whispered.

"Don't thank me. Thank God. This is all grace—or mercy—or both."

Leon nodded. "Yes, thank God. Thank God! Now I can make the rent and buy food."

What? Rent? Food?

A pain seared through Sophie's conscience. Simon's Gallery would take half of the seven thousand dollars in commission, so all Leon actually earned was thirty-five hundred dollars. How long would that last?

Forgive me, Lord Jesus. I have wronged this man. He's only trying to make ends meet.

Sophie had never been hungry in her life. There had been nothing needed that her family hadn't provided, even after college. She had been pampered.

Leon had no one—

Leon has God.

God provides.

How quickly I forget.

Her eyes stung.

"Sophie?" Leon's voice sounded anxious. "Are you okay?"

"Yeah, yeah. I'm fine. Just tired, is all. Thanks for asking."

Leon nodded. "I'll go check on your soup."

CHAPTER TWENTY

*I*n spite of their blossoming relationship, Leon still couldn't get Sophie to approve his mixed-media displays in Simon's Gallery. He decided that he should take up her advice and reduce the sheer size of his exhibits.

She had called them structures.

Well, maybe they were.

On the other hand, he could simply wait for Simon to get back to work. It had been about a month since Simon fell on the sidewalk, and he was halfway through his healing—maybe?

Leon could be patient.

Then again, he could forget the whole thing altogether.

He determined that even if Sophie vetoed his art displays, he'd still...

Love her anyway?

Love?

Leon caught himself and halted his own thoughts, as he stood by the door of Riverside Chapel, handing out the Sunday morning service programs.

He waved to Heidi Wei, entering the rented space with her brother, Ming. They lived about ten blocks from his house on Tybee Island, sharing a beach house while Heidi went to graduate school.

Leon wondered what it would feel like to have a sibling.

He had grown up alone with Mom, and had done a lot of things alone. Played alone, studied alone, went to the movies alone.

Sometimes he had been curious about his father, what he was doing these days, whether he had another family.

Whether Leon had any stepbrother or stepsister.

Then again, on most days, he didn't want to know.

In some ways, he wanted to blame his father for abandoning their family, putting Mom into a spiral that ended her life. At the same time, Leon knew he couldn't blame anyone for decisions that Mom had made on her own.

We all own our decisions.

He stared through the door to the sidewalk and cobblestones. This storefront wasn't in the center of activities on River Street, making it harder for people to find the church on Sunday mornings.

Pastor Diego Flores had said they had been discussing finding a new space to meet.

So deep was he in thought that Leon almost missed the SUV that pulled up in front of his eyes.

He put down the stack of programs immediately and went outside.

"Simon!" Leon couldn't believe he came to church this morning.

Xian and Sophie were helping him out of the SUV and into his wheelchair.

"Let me," Leon said, taking over. He was stronger than Xian, he was sure, but Sophie stepped aside anyway, going around to the back of the wheelchair to hold it.

They had locked the wheels in place, so it wasn't going anywhere, but Leon didn't say anything to Sophie.

He glanced at her. It was fleeting, but her eyes said she was happy to see him.

He remembered their sweet kiss on the beach.

As he placed Simon on his wheelchair, the elderly gentleman leaned toward him. "Not asking for favors, are you, young man?"

"Favors?" Leon was shocked at the question. "No, sir."

"He wanted to give us a hand," Xian said.

Leon nodded. "I don't expect anything in return. It's my turn to be an usher today."

"Good," Simon declared. "In spite of my earnest support for you, your *Home Life* exhibit is not happening at Simon's Gallery."

"No problem, sir. I'm putting feelers out, and some out-of-state galleries might be interested." Leon looked at Sophie. "Baxter has been texting me about options."

Sophie nodded.

"Glad to hear that," Simon said. "Now, those oil pastels... You got more of those?"

"If commissioned, I'll paint more." Leon walked ahead of Sophie, who was pushing her dad's wheelchair.

"Good answer."

Leon opened the door and held it for them to enter the temporary sanctuary.

When Simon passed by Leon, he had more to say. "My daughter doesn't like messiness. You make messy art."

"Dad." Sophie bristled.

"I take that as a compliment," Leon responded.

"She likes clean lines," Simon added. "You keep

that in mind, and more of your pieces might be displayed at the gallery."

Leon nodded. Why had Simon chosen this time to tell him all this?

"Clean, clear lines. Focus on clarity, Leon."

~

*C*larity?

What did Simon mean by that?

The question dogged Leon all the way through morning church and the entire Sunday afternoon, when he returned to his art studio and home to ponder life's great confusion.

She likes clean lines.

Leon told himself to resist trying to please Sophie. After all, she was only human. Sure, they had kissed. He had wanted it, and she hadn't resisted him.

In fact, if he recalled, Sophie had rather enjoyed their kiss on the beach.

He stood in front of his fish tank mixed-media piece, wondering what he should do.

Have you considered making smaller structures?

Leon smiled.

Sophie clearly wasn't an artist.

Why in the world did Simon make her the temporary director of his art gallery?

Even as he thought the question, Leon knew the answer.

Because Baxter would pick up the slack.

Perhaps Simon wanted Sophie to experience his work. *Like, take your daughter to work day?*

Still, Leon couldn't reconcile the two statements.

She likes clean lines.

Have you considered making smaller structures?

The word *structures* struck him.

Clearly, Sophie lived a structured life.

Leon couldn't. His life would always be one filled with fluid nonlinear lines, with splashes of color as far as the eyes could see.

He prayed silently, asking God to give him direction.

My God is never chaotic.

Everything in God's plan had a purpose and meaning, right?

Clarity.

"Lord, please clarify my purpose in life, especially my career and my relationship with..." He sighed. "Sophie."

It was too early to tell where they would go from there.

Too early to tell what Sophie thought about their being together.

Leon wanted to spend more time with her.

132

And yet...

He couldn't read her mind.

Well, that meant they needed to spend more time together.

Leon texted her, reading it aloud as he did so. "Glad your dad is back at church."

She didn't reply.

CHAPTER TWENTY-ONE

*A*fter church that evening, Sophie approached Leon to tell him she had received his text messages that afternoon. She felt that it would be better to speak to him in person.

Leon was stacking chairs in the room, but Sophie didn't offer to help since they were almost done anyway. She just followed him around.

"I'm sorry about Dad. He's too forward sometimes."

Leon smiled. "Clarity and clean lines, huh?"

"Don't let me influence your creativity."

"Since I'm creative, I can do anything," Leon declared.

Sophie didn't know whether that was in jest or whether he was serious about what he said.

"Really," Leon added.

That answered her question.

"Don't worry about me." Leon rubbed her arm with his free hand.

"I feel bad we can't display your pieces in Dad's gallery."

"Now you feel bad?" He chuckled. "No, no. Seriously, don't worry about me, okay? I'll find another gallery. In fact, I'm in contact with a couple of galleries that might be interested."

Sophie's face lit up. "Oh, I'm so glad."

"I'll have to find a way to get what you called *structures* all the way to Miami, but my ex—I mean, friend—is heading that way in a week, and she said she can come pick me up on the way."

Ex?

Sophie tried not to react. She kept her voice even. "Hope you get good sales to offset the expenses."

Leon nodded. "Say, you want to go get some coffee?"

Sophie glanced at her watch. "Not at eight o'clock at night."

"A walk then?"

Sophie hesitated. She wanted to go home and get some sleep. She had planned on getting to the gallery at the crack of dawn to go over Dad's budget. He might be a businessman, but she had already seen ways to cut costs in the gallery. And he would need it, considering the escalating expenses for his expansion.

Why in the world did Dad decide to expand a gallery that hadn't been showing a lot of profit?

"Something on your mind?" Leon asked.

Sophie wondered how much to say. How much did Leon know about Simon's Gallery?

"Something you want to talk about? I can keep secrets."

"You can?" Sophie grinned.

"But not this." Leon planted a kiss on her cheek.

Sophie reddened as a couple of church members whistled as they walked by.

Pretty soon the entire church would know that they were heading somewhere. Well, for a church this small, Sophie was surprised it hadn't been obvious.

How did this happen?

In reality, she felt swept into his arms. She remembered feeling it when she had been sitting on the rooftop patio waiting for Leon to finish painting her. Even after the shock of finding out that he had painted her into an abstract art had worn off, Sophie still felt something for Leon.

And Leon had shown her that it went both ways.

Yet she wondered why they had not kissed

anywhere else away from the beach behind his house.

~

*B*efore they were seated on the third floor of Piper's Place, Leon received a text message from a church member. He was so excited he could barely sit down on the small sofa next to Sophie.

The third floor of Piper's Place was like a giant living room, where there were multiple arrangements of cozy sitting areas surrounding coffee tables. It was as if they were at home, being served food from the kitchen.

In this relaxed atmosphere, the next piece of good news had come.

"Wow." Leon shook his head as he reread the message. Nearly wept. "Wow. God is good."

"Tell me." Sophie handed him one of the two menus the server had left them.

Leon hadn't even noticed the server come and go. His eyes were on his phone. "You know Jerome Pendegrast, who operates the two riverboats across the street?"

"The one whose salvation we've been praying for?"

"Yep. He saw the buzz about my oil pastels, and

he wants to commission me to paint some for the cabins on his riverboat."

"That's awesome. Indeed, God is good. How many is he talking about?"

"Twelve. Since he wants so many, I might have to give him a discount."

Sophie looked at him intently. "Do you?"

"Huh?"

"A discount. Did he seem to think he wants a discount?"

"I don't know. I just feel like... I don't know how I feel." Leon put away his phone. He'd have to process this first before he replied to Jerome. He didn't want to say something stupid in his excitement.

"Don't shortchange yourself," Sophie explained. "If you think your artwork is worth it, ask for a fair price."

"You didn't think my work was worth much."

"Not your *Home Life* exhibition, no."

Leon tilted his head. "I'm glad you're honest with me."

"After I got over the shock of seeing my non-portrait in two hundred colors—"

"Two hundred and twenty-one," Leon corrected her.

"Even worse! In any case, I realized that your oil

pastel painting was very vibrant. I'm glad it sold that quickly. You should do more."

"But?"

"But if Jerome is willing to pay full price, and you could use the money, it's a win-win for both of you."

"The bottom line is still the same. Can you afford to make a living?"

Leon leaned toward her. "Is that the bottom line?"

"If you're running a business, yes."

"But I'm also an artist." Leon waited for the server to take their orders—decaffeinated coffee for him and a bottle of mineral water for Sophie—before he continued speaking. "Art is more than business."

"Ah, that's why you probably could use a business manager."

"The position is open." Leon's hand touched hers. "Interested?"

"I'll pray about it."

"Good answer."

CHAPTER TWENTY-TWO

After a month of hanging out with Leon, Sophie realized in more ways than one that their picnic spot on the sandy beach behind Leon's house was his personal space that he had somehow shared with her. This was where he went to think and ponder over his life—on the same beach he had said goodbye to his mother, facing the same ocean where she had perished two years prior.

Sophie felt special about being included into his little world, even though Leon hadn't disclosed to her everything she wanted to know about him.

Sophie was looking for transparency, but Leon would only show a little bit about himself at a time.

Today she wanted to ask about his family, about his dad, who had been absent from most of his life.

She felt that he would open up if she shared a bit about her own dad.

Spearing some cut-up mixed fruits in a paper cup, Sophie wondered how to broach the subject. They had just finished their breakfast of lukewarm pancakes that Leon had made for them. She had brought a bowl of mixed fruits. Leon had finished his and was resting now.

The November morning was cool around them. Sophie had put on a cardigan, but the breeze was still a bit chilly. All around them she could hear seabirds and the ocean. Growing up in Savannah and on Tybee Island, she was used to the sounds of the ocean. These days, with so much on her mind, the ocean had become part of her backdrop, a faded background.

"Want some more coffee?" Sophie asked.

"No, thanks." Leon was lying down on the picnic blanket, sunglasses over his eyes.

He wasn't wearing plaid today. In fact, he was in a worn-and-torn, faded, once-brown, long-sleeved tee shirt that would've been a rag cloth on Sophie's kitchen floor. It looked very comfortable though.

"Something on your mind?"

"Dad's getting better," Sophie said.

"Good. Prayers work."

"God works."

"Yes." He lifted up his sunglasses. "I can tell from your voice that you're thinking about the gallery."

"You can't tell."

"Can too." He sat up.

"What am I thinking then? Details, please?"

"Clean lines."

"Meaning what?" Sophie asked. "Really, tell me."

"If you prefer clean lines, then it makes sense that you dislike my mixed-media art pieces."

"Well..."

Leon put up a palm. "Let me finish."

Sophie waited.

"If you prefer clarity, then you'd be wondering why your dad bought the empty building next door to the gallery. The purpose is nebulous. There's no clarity."

"Only mold." Sophie finished the last piece of mixed fruit. She put down the paper cup.

"That too." He reached for her.

That was one thing about Leon that Sophie found interesting. He had to touch her somehow. It was as if that was his language. To get his points across, it wasn't enough for him to speak. He had to use his hands.

Even on the first day they had spoken to each

other at the gallery, Leon had held her hand when he led her to the army cot, where she had taken a nap.

"What's on your mind?" Leon asked softly.

"I want to help Dad," Sophie said. "I am thinking of suggesting to him that he use the space next door for art classes. I'm not an artist, so I don't know if that's a good idea. Will the returns be worth the investment?"

"He's already paying for the building."

"True."

"He could pay the art teachers a percentage of the class fees. That way he doesn't have to put them on salary."

"No healthcare, then."

Leon shrugged. "They're on their own. Such is life."

"So the more art classes he has, the more everyone earns."

"Would it be enough to pay for the building?" Sophie asked.

"A long shot maybe. But it keeps the building occupied."

Sophie brushed curls off her face and pulled the cardigan tighter around herself.

"If you're cold, we can go inside," Leon said.

"Or we'll bring a wool blanket next time."

"That's an idea too."

Sophie looked into the distance. The Saturday sunshine brightened the entire beach, but the brightness was deceiving. She was sure the temperature wasn't going to break into the sixties today.

"I'm going to come up with a possible plan and talk to Dad at lunch today," Sophie said.

"Pray over the plan," Leon suggested.

"I think it's a good plan, but you're right about prayer. I need all the prayer I can get. Sometimes I don't know if the idea is mine or whether it comes from God."

"I hear you. I'm in the same boat."

"Truly, I don't know how to best help Dad. He's not suffering or anything—financially—but he's in his late seventies, almost eighty, and here he is, expanding a gallery... Oh, I shouldn't tell you all that."

"I already knew about it."

Sophie was surprised. She waited for Leon to tell her more.

"Your dad told me he wondered if he'd made a mistake buying the building next door."

"When?"

"A month after."

"He didn't tell me."

"You were busy working, I think?" Leon said, as

if he didn't want Sophie to know that he knew a lot more about her than he was letting on.

"What else did Dad tell you about me?" Curious now.

"Only good things." He patted her knee. "He says you write obscure user guides that nobody reads and engineering manuals for little-used heavy machinery."

Sophie laughed. "He said all that?"

"He said you're a creative person but you never had a chance."

Sophie hung her head. "I'm so deprived."

"Do you like your job?" Leon asked.

Stunned, Sophie didn't reply. That could be telling, she thought. *Do I like my job?*

"Do you enjoy your job?" he tried again.

"It pays the bills," Sophie managed.

It was all she wanted to say. *So who's not being transparent now?*

"I love my job," Leon offered. "It may not pay as much as yours, but the freedom is worth the price of admission. I spent so many mornings on the deck of Jerome's riverboat, painting the river scene."

"How many have you completed?"

"Two. Tomorrow after church, he's letting me into one of the cabins so I can see where the paintings are going to be hung."

"Good for you. I'm happy to hear that things are

going well for you." Sophie shifted. "I need to get up."

Leon stood up and pulled Sophie to her feet. They walked along the ocean's edge.

"I'm going to take your suggestion and downsize my mixed-media creations," Leon said.

"You are?" *How nice.*

"It's a good idea. I'm always open to good ideas."

Sophie nodded. *Am I open to good ideas?*

"God has been doing some amazing things in my life." Leon interlocked his fingers into Sophie's. "I've been wandering in the desert for two years, and now I'm in an oasis."

Sophie smiled.

"My art is finally paying off," Leon explained. "And it's because the Lord brought you into my life."

"Me?"

"If you hadn't agreed to sit for the portrait, I wouldn't have painted it, it wouldn't have sold, and no one would have commissioned me for more of it, paying full price."

"God worked it all out for your good."

"For *our* good."

"Our good? Because now you're not mad at me that I made you remove your *Home Life* exhibit from the gallery?"

"Well, I'm sort of still getting over that." Leon

ran his hands up and down her arms. "I need a kiss to make it all better."

Sophie pulled away and began to run. "Only if you can catch me."

Leon laughed and chased after her.

CHAPTER TWENTY-THREE

"*A*n educational space, huh?" Dad rubbed his stubbled jaw. He was relaxing on the couch, wearing his favorite at-home sweatshirt with a wool blanket covering his legs.

They had just eaten lunch that Sophie had helped Xian prepare. It was a simple meal of shrimp fried rice and tossed salad. For dessert, they had Dad's favorite cheesecake.

Sophie wasn't sure how cheesecake went with fried rice, but there they were. She eased her full tummy into a recliner across the coffee table from Dad's couch.

In the kitchen, Xian was on the phone with her sister in Taiwan, chattering away in Mandarin Chinese.

"There are two floors, right?" Sophie asked Dad.

"We could put exhibits on the first floor." Dad seemed to warm up to the idea. "And make the second floor an art education space. Or the other way around. Either way, it seems kinda tight."

"Not really. If you hire artists like Abilene Dupree, she paints outdoors."

"Good point. So the classes could be under the trees, on the beach, et cetera."

Sophie nodded. "I don't know how much you'll earn, but if you can get students from the Savannah Senior Living Resort..."

"Ah yes." Dad perked up. "They're retired. Art could be a hobby."

"Uh-huh."

"Have you talked to Abilene?" Dad asked.

"No. It's your gallery."

"It's your idea." Dad folded his arms across his blanket. "You ask Abilene, and I'll ask Leon."

"Leon?" Sophie waited to see what Dad was up to.

"He could teach sculpting and mixed media."

Oh dear. "As long as he keeps the structures small."

Dad burst out laughing. "Structures?"

"Is there any other way to describe them?"

Xian came into the room. "Describe what?"

"Leon's *Home Life* pieces." Dad pointed to Sophie. "She calls them *structures*."

"I don't think he cares what she calls them." Xian sat on another armchair near Dad. "I saw the way he looks at you at church. He's in love."

Leon?

In love?

Sophie blinked. So when had they gone past *like?*

~

"*You* ou always like to do things for the people you love," Sophie's brother said on the phone.

Love?

That word again.

Sophie closed the sliding glass door leading to her tiny patio. There was nothing to see outside but a brick wall. The Saturday afternoon sunlight shone down at an oblique angle, but the magnolia tree next door absorbed most of it.

She wished she had never bought this townhouse.

It looked like a cat's litter box compared to Leon's house on the beach. So much open space there...

Leon?

Why am I thinking of Leon?

"You'd do the same for Dad if you were here."

Sophie settled into her Ikea futon. It was new, and it doubled up as a guest bed when her brother Adam came to town, though he hadn't been to Savannah lately.

In fact, Sophie didn't always know where Adam was. His work with the U.S. Marshals Service took him everywhere, and he never called home from work.

"I'm not sure if I'd take two months off." Adam laughed. "You're the only one willing to do that."

"Xian needs help, and you know how needy Dad is."

"So he's getting better, I gather?"

"Still in cast." Sophie nodded, though it was meaningless across the many miles between them. "His shinbone is healing. I think he'll be back at work very soon."

Sophie was glad she wasn't driving Dad back and forth to the doctor. It would be quite a drive to hear him moan and groan and complain. "Pray that Dad will get well soon."

"The sooner the better, huh?"

"For everyone."

"I have to go, but before I do, I want to tell you about a verse I read the other day," Adam said.

"Yeah?" Sophie liked listening to what her brother had learned from the Bible.

"It describes you, you know? Philippians 2:3."

Adam seemed to be reading. "See what it says here. 'Let nothing be done through selfish ambition or conceit, but in lowliness of mind let each esteem others better than himself.' I need that reminder myself."

"Good verse. Then again, every verse in the Bible is good."

"That's you, Sophie. You esteem a lot of people better than yourself."

"I don't know..."

"Remember what I always remind you?"

"Yeah. Got it." But she knew her brother would repeat it anyway.

"Do something for yourself for once."

"I'd rather please God than myself," Sophie countered.

What her brother hadn't realized all this time was that Sophie was the happiest when she could make others happy...

Except Leon.

Was he happy now with his oil pastel artwork that had sold?

It wasn't his first love, apparently, considering the only such paintings he had done were that one he painted of her and the new commissioned pieces for Jerome Pendegrast's riverboats.

Commissioned.

It seemed that Leon would rather be a free artist, creating whatever he wanted.

Sophie felt sorry now that she had removed his displays from the gallery. What if there were people out there who liked his type of art?

She hated to second-guess her own decision, but it had been influenced by all those years of tagging along with Dad to art galleries everywhere—not just here in North America but also in Europe.

Sophie liked to think she knew what was good for Dad's gallery.

Especially since Dad had confidence in her.

Which explained why Dad hadn't protested much, even though he had thought he could save Leon's artwork if he let him have the new space next door.

Whatever.

In two months, Dad could have the gallery back, and he could do whatever he wanted.

That decision to remove Leon's work had bothered Sophie, but she felt better after she had tried to compensate him for the decision.

She had asked Baxter to help Leon find a gallery to display his...stuff.

She had agreed to let Leon paint a portrait of her—and it had led to a windfall income for him.

And she had accepted his invitations to picnics on the beach.

Well, because she wanted to.

And it had made him happy.

Does it make me happy?

That wasn't the issue, was it? She only wanted to please God. And if helping someone else pleased God, then she would do it.

It was no sacrifice for her.

Not after what Jesus Christ had done for her on the cross.

But the kisses—they were not part of her helpfulness...

Sophie's fingers went to her lips.

She had indeed felt something more for Leon, and she knew he felt the same way toward her as well.

Was this the beginning of love between a man and a woman?

Funny, all her old past dates and boyfriends had not been like Leon.

With Leon she had almost known from the day he walked into the gallery that he was different. Sure, they had passed by each other at church— without speaking—and he had known Dad.

Dad and Xian seemed to like him. They had nothing bad to say about him at all.

In fact, Xian asked me if I liked Leon.

Had it been that obvious?

CHAPTER TWENTY-FOUR

On Sunday morning, Pastor Diego Flores spoke about resting in the peace of the Lord. It was the last thing Leon could think of at this hour, and he was getting antsy in his seat as his pastor read John 16:33 aloud.

"Listen to the words of Jesus. 'These things I have spoken to you, that in Me you may have peace. In the world you will have tribulation; but be of good cheer, I have overcome the world.' Friends, God has encouraged us."

Pastor Flores paused, as if to wait for the congregation to keep up.

"In this world, you will have problems. The word 'will' implies a future tense," he added. "However, Jesus has overcome the world. That's in the past tense. He has already done it."

"Fellow Christians, when the Bible tells you to 'be of good cheer' and then tells you why, you can have assurance that God is going to take care of it—whatever it might be." Pastor Flores seemed to be looking his way, but Leon tried not to read too much into his facial expression.

How in the world was Leon going to "be of good cheer" when he was upset?

His first mistake this morning was to check his email in between Sunday School and the church service, and finding a tweet from Cholandra, who had tagged his Twitter handle. He had almost deleted the notification.

His second mistake had been to entertain his own curiosity. He had read the linked article. Key phrases stabbed his heart like daggers from beyond the grave.

Sea Islands Symphony Orchestra.

Conductor Bouvier Petrocelli.

Savannah Christmas Concert Series.

Save the dates, my foot.

"We have faith in God. We trust that God is going to work it out," Pastor Flores continued. "In Christ, we have peace. In Christ, we overcome."

How could Leon "have peace" when everything in him burned against the name in the article that Cholandra had tweeted?

How could he overcome this mess when everything was a trigger today?

As the sermon went on, Leon felt less and less optimistic, even as Pastor Flores's message was upbeat—to some.

"Where is our peace? In Christ," Pastor Flores repeated. "How do we overcome? In Christ."

In Christ.

Somehow Leon didn't feel close to Christ right now. That email from Cholandra continued to bug him.

As the sermon went on, Leon felt less thankful, less at peace, as if his circumstances had now overcome him instead of the other way around. The concert flyer flapped in his mind. He could see the words in front of him, blocking him from listening to the full sermon.

Symphony Orchestra.

Conductor Bouvier Petrocelli.

If words could make him angry, those did it.

Even worse was the thought that his own middle name was Bouvier.

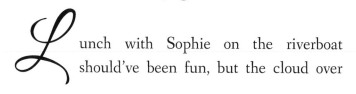

*L*unch with Sophie on the riverboat should've been fun, but the cloud over

Leon's past had threatened that special hour with someone he loved.

Loved?

How could he love her right now, in the midst of this dark past that the cat had dragged in? Never mind that he had blown a big chunk of this month's budget on this lunch.

He wanted to do it for Sophie.

They went through the buffet lunch pretty quickly, and Sophie did a lot of the talking. She seemed oblivious to the pain in his chest.

"That was a good sermon, wasn't it?" Sophie said, sitting down with a second helping of chicken or something.

"Huh?"

"Pastor Flores's sermon." Sophie laughed. "Don't tell me you fell asleep."

Sophie had been on nursery duty that morning, and she must've listened to part of the sermon through the live camera and speakers in the playroom.

Leon had sat alone, and as he recalled—somewhat shamefully—he had pouted the entire time.

"I'm an orphan," he declared suddenly.

"Is your dad dead?" Sophie asked.

Dad. The last person he wanted to talk about. "He might as well have been."

"He's still alive, right?" Sophie pointed a fork at him. "Technically, you can't be an orphan."

"Look here. I'm trying to have a pity party."

"Based on a false premise." Sophie finished her seconds. "What's your dad's name?"

"You sure can eat a lot." As for Leon, he could hardly take another bite. His appetizer was still half-eaten. Forget the main meal or dessert.

He had no appetite right now.

He should've canceled their reservation, but he couldn't do it when he saw Sophie being excited after church to have lunch with him on the riverboat.

"You're changing the subject, Leon," Sophie said. "And that bad mood of yours is messing up this beautiful Sunday on the river."

Silence.

"Is there any problem God cannot solve?" Sophie asked.

"He may not want to solve this one."

"Nothing is impossible with God. Haven't you heard that over and over again?"

"Everywhere. But."

"*But* is a bad word when it comes to questioning God."

"Like I said, He may not want to solve this one."

"That's up to Him, isn't it?" Sophie reminded

him. "So. Did something happen this morning at church?"

"Twitter notified me that someone tagged me in a retweet."

"Okay. I get that a lot from my friends from everywhere."

"It was from my ex—just a friend."

"Your ex-girlfriend?" Sophie asked, her face changing slightly.

"Look—I'm not still in touch with her, not in a personal way. She gives me leads on galleries that might want to show my work. Like that gallery in Miami. I need that for business."

Sophie didn't reply.

Leon wondered if she was ever the jealous sort. Six weeks weren't enough to know in-depth about a person. However, Simon had told him about Sophie. Said that she was one of the most giving and charitable persons in their entire Kowalski family.

Xian had even added more tidbits about Sophie that warmed up Leon's heart. For instance, at one point in her college years, Sophie had given up pursuing a classmate because her best friend had also been interested in the same guy.

Self-sacrificing?

He wondered if Sophie would step aside if Cholandra wanted him back.

He reached for her hand across the table. "The

point is that I don't want to be reminded of my father, and Cholandra had done that, and it made me very angry."

"Still makes you angry."

"Well, being with you helps."

"How long ago did your dad leave you?"

"I'm almost twenty-nine. So I'd say it has been twenty-seven years? Something like that."

Sophie pulled her hand back from Leon. She folded her arms. "Twenty-seven years of anger?"

"I don't know when I started getting angry with him."

"I'm going to guess that it came to head when you saw your mom suffer alone."

Mom.

She did suffer alone.

For many years.

Leon held back a tear. "Ah..."

He couldn't speak.

He covered his face with the cloth napkin.

"If you want to go, we can leave," Sophie said quietly.

Leon nodded.

CHAPTER TWENTY-FIVE

*T*hey left Leon's car at the parking lot near Riverside Chapel, where there was no fee for Sunday parking. Sophie felt that Leon was in no condition to drive.

It was radio silence in the car all the way to Tybee Island, where the November afternoon temperature peaked at a miserable forty-five degrees.

Still, Sophie knew that the beach behind Leon's house was his comfort zone, and she wanted to take him there. She wanted to stay with him until they went back to church that evening.

She prayed for her own self that she would not be paranoid.

Somewhere in the back of her mind, she was

afraid that Leon would be too depressed to think straight.

Twenty-seven years of deep sorrow about an absentee dad could turn into something dark and ugly.

Sophie herself had experienced anguish about her own mother's death, but she had died at childbirth. She had not taken her own life.

What a contrast.

Leon's mom had been a Christian, and yet she had taken her own life.

Sophie's mom had been unsaved, and yet she had perished too early.

The ironies of life.

So how was it that Sophie had weathered the pain better than Leon?

Perhaps, in spite of how difficult Dad had been, he had done his best. And his best had been enough to raise Sophie and her brother, both now leading productive lives and making their dad proud.

Neither spoke a word as Sophie's car rolled to a stop in front of Leon's rental house. She applied the parking brakes and turned to look at Leon.

His eyes were still red. "I need to change."

"I'll wait out back."

"You don't want to come in?"

"I'm going to sit in the sun and talk to God."

Leon nodded.

Sophie took off her shoes and walked barefoot around the house to the beach. When she crossed over the dunes, there was nothing to sit on, so she went to the edge of the ocean, being careful not to let the salt water get to her wool dress pants.

The roar of the ocean was loud, reminding her that life went on.

Even in the afternoon sun, her outfit looked dark.

Like she was still in mourning.

Am I?

I shouldn't be.

Mom had been gone a good twenty-six years. It was time to let her go, the same way Leon had let his own mother go that Monday morning about a month ago. Their mothers had died at different times of their lives.

And yet they had each dealt with their situations a bit differently.

Perhaps it was because Sophie never knew her mother. It had been easier for her.

Oddly, Leon hadn't been grieving for his mom, though she had been with him most of his life.

It was his father who had been the pain in his life.

Funny how life was. People alive could sometimes cause the most hurt.

"Lord Jesus, give me the right words to say," Sophie whispered in the wind, her voice mingling with the crashing waves. "Let everything I do be pleasing to you."

The wind whipped at her face. She wished she had tied up her hair, which was now dancing wildly in the air.

"His name is Bouvier Petrocelli." Leon's voice came from behind her.

It was a sure voice, Sophie thought.

A good first step for him to even mention his absentee father's name.

Sophie prayed quickly on how to respond. She turned around to find Leon in the same plaid shirt he had worn the first day they had talked to each other in the art gallery.

For a moment, she was distracted. "I like that shirt."

"I just told you my father's name."

"Yes. It's going to be okay. I prayed about it. God will get us through this."

"Thank you for praying." He held out his hand.

Sophie leaned into Leon's arms.

The shirt smelled like fresh laundry.

She closed her eyes.

"I gather you like this shirt," Leon said.

"I like the one wearing it."

Leon looked into her eyes. "Like? Not love?"

"We could get there eventually."

"I might be there already," Leon confessed. "But you'll need to give me time to be worthy of honoring you."

"Only God is worthy, Leon."

"I have baggage, as you can tell."

Sophie held Leon's hand and urged him to walk with her along the edge of the world. "Remember what you told me one of the times we were here?"

"I said many things."

"You said that the Bible calls us to honor our parents, even if they have issues."

Leon was quiet. Then: "Was that when you told me your dad is difficult?"

"Was. But he could still be. I don't know, since I don't live with him anymore. That's Xian's burden to bear. But he did his best, you know?"

"I guess so."

"You also said that you were thankful to God for saving our souls through Jesus."

"Thankful. Grateful." Leon put his arm around Sophie's waist. "What Pastor Flores preached this morning..."

"John 6:33. 'In the world you will have tribulation; but be of good cheer, I have overcome the world.' That verse?"

"You know your verses," Leon remarked.

"Because that was one of those important verses we had to memorize back in youth group—years ago."

"How quickly we forget."

"And how quickly we fail to apply to our present situation." Sophie stopped. "What do you think God wants us to do?"

"Us? This is my problem, not yours."

"I've lost a parent too. I've been there. I hear you."

Leon resumed walking, and Sophie had to go along.

"We each have our own ways of dealing with problems," Leon said.

"Yet God is still the same, no matter what. I think He'd want us to respond to problems in such a way that we can attach the Name of Jesus to it—like a stamp of approval—and in such a way that shows our thankfulness to God through Jesus."

"Wow. That's a sermonette."

"I've learned a lot studying my Bible and going to church and attending Bible studies."

"Good for you."

They walked further in silence. Then they stopped to look out across the ocean.

All Sophie could think of was how far the Atlantic went. That the horizon was so far away.

There was something about it, but she couldn't see the meaning of it now.

"I don't want to share this burden with you." Leon's voice vibrated into the wind, but Sophie heard him loudly and clearly.

"What are you saying?" Sophie searched his eyes. "We're in this together."

"This is not your albatross."

"What albatross?" Sophie was alarmed. "This is real life."

"Forgive me for causing you concern."

"Don't worry about it."

Leon put both hands gently on Sophie's shoulders. "I have something to ask you later."

"Yes?"

"Later."

"Later may never come," Sophie said. Still, she did not press for the question.

Leon quietly and gently cupped Sophie's face in his hands. His warm hands.

Sophie closed her eyes as she felt his lips touch hers.

His warm lips against her cold ones.

His hesitant kiss turned more assured and more secure when Sophie wrapped her arms around Leon's taut waist.

The beach seemed to warm up around Sophie,

even as Tybee Island winds whistled and the Atlantic Ocean played a chorus that came and went.

It was a different kind of warmth she was feeling now.

A strange warmth that said both *hello* and *goodbye* at the same time.

CHAPTER TWENTY-SIX

"*N*ot a word?" Xian gasped, staring at Sophie's dad.

Dad remained silent.

Above them, the screened-in porch fan thwacked. All around them, the sounds of Savannah faded away as Sophie grappled with her situation.

She tried to contain herself. "Not a word, and it's Thursday."

"One week before Thanksgiving," Xian added.

Dad bristled, as if trying to tell Xian not to rub it in. Xian seemed oblivious to his body language.

If this were a normal day, Sophie would've found it funny.

Not today.

Today she was sad and upset at the same time. If she dug deeper into her heart, she might find anger

ASK YOU LATER

in there too—she was sure of it—for Leon's emotional actions.

Still, gone is gone.

The last time Sophie had seen and talked to Leon was Sunday.

Sitting on a rattan chair in one corner of her parents' porch adjacent to Dad's chair, she had been keeping an eye on her iPhone. Riverside Chapel had been mobilized to pray for Leon.

Everyone was sure he had left them for reasons of his own. As a grown adult, there was nothing stopping him from leaving.

Leon had not returned anyone's calls. Almost everyone he knew from Riverside Chapel had tried to contact him by email, text, phone, and social media.

No response.

Ming had talked to the landlady. Leon had left no forwarding address. Ming's PI firm could not get any information from Leon's bank, and it wasn't a case for the police to get involved. Yet.

Ming's friend Camden La Salle worked for the FBI and could help at the national level. Camden attended Riverside Chapel as well, but he was currently on an assignment out of town.

Sophie dared not entertain the worst option possible, that perhaps Leon had killed himself.

No.

171

Please, Lord Jesus, sustain him.

"If he needs time alone, doesn't he need to tell you?" Xian asked.

"We're dating, but we're not engaged or married," Sophie rationalized. "It would be nice and polite of him to tell me he needs space or something, but he was behaving oddly on Sunday, like he was in grief."

"I just don't get it," Xian continued. "I thought Leon was over it. Wasn't he getting any grief counseling from Pastor Flores?"

Dad shifted in his outdoor lounge chair. "He attended the group meetings that Pastor Flores conducts at the Savannah Senior Living Resort for children of residents who passed away."

"Isn't there some sort of custom grief counseling?" Sophie asked.

"Yes, but Leon didn't want to do any one on one."

"Too painful, I think?" Xian offered.

Sophie shrugged. Dad had told her Leon's story as soon as she arrived at their house at lunch to report that Leon had left town.

It had been an old story, and Sophie was attending another church at that time, nearly two years ago. When she had moved membership from the Pooler church to Riverside Chapel, it had been months before Leon returned to Savannah from his travels around the world.

It seemed that he had needed that time away to gather his thoughts and come to grips with his mother's death.

It had all made sense now.

"Dad, if Leon needed encouragement, why did you let me cancel his art exhibition?" Sophie asked.

She wished she hadn't interfered.

"Because it's time for Leon to deal with real life," Dad said slowly. "But..."

"But?"

"He fell in love with you."

"Not so, Dad. If he is in love with me, why did he run away?"

"Cold feet?"

"And what does he expect me to do? Carry on? Forget we ever met?"

"Something must've triggered it," Dad said. "I've talked to Pastor Flores about his past, and all we can do now is to pray, pray, pray."

"For what, Dad?" Sophie wiped her eyes.

Usually she was able to hold it in, but today, it was harder than other times.

Am I in love with Leon?

Is that why my heart hurts this much?

"Pray for God's perfect will to be done." Dad's hand reached for Sophie's.

She let him hold it. It was her childhood all over again, when Dad had to be two parents to her all through her life.

"God is always sovereign, yes?" Dad reminded her. "Let's pray now."

Bowing their heads, holding hands, Sophie let Dad pray for Leon, for them, for God to deal with the situation in Leon's heart. It was beyond them, for sure, but nothing was beyond God.

When Sophie opened her eyes, she saw that her tears had splashed onto the surface of her iPhone on her lap. She wiped the screen on the edge of her dress shirt. The screen came alive and told her it was almost two o'clock in the afternoon.

"I'd better get back to the gallery," Sophie said.

Dad shook his head. "I texted Baxter at lunch. He's keeping an eye on things. I want you to take the afternoon off."

"Not much of an afternoon, is it?" Sophie tried to smile. Her face felt tight, like she was wearing a mask.

A mask of tears.

Really, she had to wash her face. The tears were getting sticky.

I probably look awful.

"I don't like the way he handles things," Sophie said. "His emotional baggage is affecting our rela-tionship."

"We all handle things differently, don't we?" Dad asked.

"I may not want him back."

"Ah, then you're doing the same thing he is— reacting emotionally."

"How else can I look at this? Who'd walk away in the middle of something beautiful?"

"Well, my dear, Leon did."

"He said he has something to ask me later," Sophie added. "Does that mean he had planned this departure?"

"Let's not think too much about it," Dad said. "We need to leave it to God, or our heads will explode with speculations. We don't know what Leon is thinking."

With Dad's words, the porch quieted again.

Sophie closed her eyes. The sting of salty tears was messing with her contact lenses. "I need to go home. I have a headache."

"How about staying for a few days in our guest room?" Xian asked.

"I don't want to impose. You have your hands full with a diff—uh, Dad."

"Hey!" Dad made a face. "Were you going to say I'm a difficult patient?"

Xian laughed. "Stay, Sophie dear. We can talk about things, have tea, pray together."

Sophie liked the idea. But... "I think I need to be alone for a little bit."

"All right," Xian said. "Don't cook. Eat dinner here."

Sophie nodded, thanking God for her family.

Family.

Poor Leon. He must think he has none.

CHAPTER TWENTY-SEVEN

*M*onday and Tuesday had been a blur to Leon. Vaguely, he remembered the seven hours of driving to Miami on Monday. And the art exhibition the next day on Miami Beach, in which he had sold nothing.

By Wednesday, Leon wondered what on earth he was doing so far away from home.

Home?

Where is home?

A picnic blanket in the morning hours on Tybee Island?

Memories of a deceased mother and an absentee father?

Ah, perhaps he'd better not go home.

Feeling transient, Leon had left his luggage

unpacked. This wasn't his house. Cholandra had been kind to offer him a place to stay. He had hesitated. He didn't want to be a third wheel, but he had no money to spare.

The house had several bedrooms, with the entire basement space dedicated to Cholandra's art studio. Leon's ex had done well for herself as an artist. He wondered why she even needed to tour the country.

Cholandra's live-in boyfriend was also her manager, and Leon didn't ask more about him, though he wondered what had happened to the once shy, Bible-toting Cholandra from high school, who had gone to every mission trip and evangelism outreach their church youth group had organized.

Now she didn't go to church at all, and she had been living with her boyfriend for at least a year.

Could I wander that far away from my own faith?

Leon felt out of place.

Not only spiritually but also environmentally. It was awkward for him to be there at all, eating free dinners, using air conditioning that someone else paid for, and being privy to Cholandra's private life.

So he had spent the last two days cooped up in her basement studio. Well, she'd called it her terrace level. The entire studio was full of natural light, being open to the backyard that led to a pool and the boat dock.

Leon was still in the middle of finishing the oil pastel paintings for Jerome Pendegrast's riverboat in Savannah. He had quit his job at Piper's Place.

He had wanted to keep renting the beach house for another month until he figured out what to do next, but the landlady told him that it was time for her to sell the house. She had gotten tired of managing rental properties.

Leon ended up renting a storage unit outside Savannah to store his artwork while he hung out with Cholandra in Miami.

Sounds of boats from the waterway reached his ears, and Leon looked up from the painting he was working on for Jerome. This would be Leon's ninth oil pastel painting. Three more to go, and he would keep his end of the deal.

He put down the pastel sticks. He stared at his fingers and palms, covered with pigments of all colors.

The colors reminded him of Sophie Kowalski.

Whom he had left behind in Savannah.

Somewhere in the back of his mind, he was sure that leaving her without a goodbye had been a bad idea. Uprooting and leaving the country had worked two years before, but now he felt different, as though it was finally time to settle down.

If he had stayed in Savannah, he would finish the commissioned paintings sooner.

He would have income from Piper's Place.

And he would have his breakfast picnic with Sophie every Saturday.

Sophie.

The one I want to be with.

He knew they wouldn't always agree on art.

Then again, life was more than art. Sophie would be the first to make it known to him, just by her art preferences.

I think I love her.

But it was too late now, wasn't it?

Leon had failed her. He had run away.

Again.

Now he was stuck in warm Miami, living in someone else's house, using someone else's studio, eating someone else's food...

And staring at his own empty life.

～

"You want, I'll track him down and beat him up." Aidan Ming Wei said it so earnestly that Sophie almost believed that Heidi's brother had meant every single word he just said.

In their usual booth at Piper's Place this late Wednesday afternoon, Sophie had lost all her appetite except for Piper's exceptional cupcakes.

Pumpkin and spice and everything nice.

Perfect for this overcast day.

Sophie folded her arms across her chest. No words formed in her head. She drew a blank as she listened to Heidi and her brother, sitting on the other side of the table. At this side of the table, Sophie sat next to Abilene Dupree, the potential new art teacher for Dad's new art education wing at the gallery.

"If he meant to leave on his own accord, it would be a waste of money to track him down," Abilene said. "He has done it before, so he might do it again."

"Dad told me about that." Sophie recalled her conversation with Dad and Xian on Tuesday. "Truly, I didn't see signs of anything, really. From my interaction with him the last two months, I felt he was working to make ends meet, like everybody else, you know?"

"Artists can be emotional people," Abilene said. "Ask me how I know."

Sophie turned to her. "You don't seem to operate by emotions."

"That's because I'm too busy." Abilene laughed.

"Besides, while being emotional is one thing, practicing emotional Christianity might not end well," Heidi said.

"We know that, but does Leon?" her brother asked. "For that matter, don't we all have logs in our own eyes?"

Everyone nodded.

Sophie finished her cupcake and ordered another one.

Heidi eyed her.

Sophie ignored it. She drank up her entire glass of iced tea.

"Girl—" Heidi started to say.

Ming put up a hand to stop her from saying more. "Someone ought to tell Leon to stop running."

"Or run to God. Run to Christ," Sophie added.

Even as she said it, Sophie realized the reminder was for herself.

Run to God.

Run to Christ.

Pastor Diego Flores's sermon from Sunday morning came to her mind. The verse from John 16:33 that he had read aloud to the Riverside Chapel congregation was now front and center. An instruction from God regarding dealing with Leon?

These things I have spoken unto you, that in Me ye might have peace. In the world ye shall have tribu-

lation: but be of good cheer; I have overcome the world.

Sophie's heart lifted. Her pain was still there, but comforting her was the peace of God.

In Christ, we are overcomers.

Thank You, Jesus.

CHAPTER TWENTY-EIGHT

When Leon arrived at the Raymond Fordham Art Studio, he found his friend at his pottery wheel, making what looked like either a round bowl or another teapot.

Leon nodded to him when he looked up from his spinning wheel. That man could make pottery with his eyes closed.

"You're early today," Raymond said.

"Yeah. I didn't come here until the afternoon yesterday, and ran out of time trying to dry my pieces."

"Nothing like the hot sun."

"Thank you for letting me use your studio," Leon said.

"No problem."

Leon had promised to teach a couple of art

classes, but Raymond didn't have enough students to make a difference or to best use his time. There were irregular streams of tourists and the occasional groups of schoolkids, but not this week.

"You know where the back-door key is?" Raymond asked.

Leon nodded, walking through the doorless frame to get to the back of the studio. Past a small kitchen on one side and shelves of pottery on the other side, Leon found the back-door key hanging near a stack of washbowls that had collected dust.

He wondered about the percentage of sales Raymond earned every year, and hoped that his own presence at the studio hadn't been a hardship for Raymond.

Well, he wasn't here to use Raymond's firing kiln or pottery wheels. He was only here to borrow that Caribbean sunshine in the backyard to dry his new mixed-media pieces before shipping them to art galleries that agreed to display them.

Next to the back door, lining up against the wall and stacked in twos, were his new miniature *Home Life Too* exhibit pieces.

Thanks to Sophie Kowalski's suggestions back in October, Leon had scaled down his mixed-media creations to fit into UPS and FedEx shipping boxes at sizes affordable to his rapidly shrinking bank account.

His last paychecks had been from Jerome Pendegrast for all twelve of the oil pastel paintings he now hung in the staterooms of his riverboat. There had been no more commissioned works since then.

All he had left was to try to revive his *Home Life* exhibition.

Revive?

Not the right word.

The right word was *launch*.

For all practical purposes, he had a failed launch when Sophie canceled his contract at Simon's Gallery. In a twist of irony, he had fallen in love with her—

Have I?

Have I really?

"Need any help?" Raymond's voice came closer.

"Sure." Leon unlocked the door and was immediately greeted by the warm midmorning heat of the Bahamas.

Raymond's studio was in a landlocked side of town, away from the coastline, a bit outside Nassau. There were no ocean breezes here, only heat from the sun above. The ocean was some thirty minutes away, but Leon couldn't remember which direction it was.

He had walked here from his dinky cottage that Raymond's sister had rented to him for a month. After this month, he had no idea where he'd go.

Leon wasn't sure if he wanted to travel around the world again.

Been there, done that.

Truly, he had thought that when he went home to Savannah about seven or eight months ago, that he'd stay for good. He wished he hadn't reacted to Cholandra's email about his long-lost dad surfacing as a critically acclaimed conductor of a symphony orchestra.

He had done the only thing he knew to do: run.

And he wished he could tell Sophie that it had nothing to do with her. He wasn't trying to leave her or hide from her or her dad. They could find him here in Nassau if they wanted to.

Yet no one had cared, had they?

Leon had been here for exactly a week since his stay in Miami—and a week and a half since he had left Savannah—and nobody had bothered to contact him.

That I know of.

He had sold his car for next to nothing and had bought a one-way plane ticket to the Bahamas, where his potter friend, Raymond, had offered him a barter for the use of his studio in Nassau.

He had left no forwarding addresses, since the landlady had told him she was selling the property.

He had also used a post office box in Miami as his business address, and Cholandra as his contact in the United States. Whenever someone asked about *Home Life Too*, she would send a note to his new email address. Then Leon would borrow Raymond's cell phone to make the call.

If Sophie or her dad or anyone else would like to track him down, they could. Leon wondered if Ming hadn't already started the search.

No need to worry.

Nobody had knocked on his door.

Leon propped open the back door with a piece of brick. The tropical air growled into his face—promising humidity at noon, and sunburn by five o'clock.

He went back inside to pick up *The Laundry Too*. He pointed to a lighter piece that Raymond could carry. Leon was aware that Raymond sometimes had problems with his lower back.

Raymond followed behind with *More Laundry Too*.

They placed the two pieces on a bench near the outdoor kiln.

Leon glanced up to find the sun behind some clouds. From the feel of it, he thought his home-made glue would dry today. There had been no forecast of rain, as he remembered from listening to the radio news this morning.

He stared at his colorful creations. They were Caribbean bright, brighter than the originals he had in storage on Tybee Island.

Leon chuckled as he wondered what Sophie would think about these new names he had given his downsized creations.

Ah, she probably hates them in any size.

He frowned.

"Is it really that bad?" Raymond asked.

Leon wasn't sure how true-to-self he was wearing his facial expression. He hadn't looked in the mirror in days. He hadn't shaved. Hadn't taken care of himself much.

"Something—someone—on your mind?" Raymond tried again.

Silence.

"Someone you left behind?"

"It's a long story."

"She pregnant?"

"Oh no, no, no." Leon bristled. "The most we've done is talk."

"Really?"

"Really."

"Well, good for you." Raymond opened the door of the nearby kiln. "You miss her?"

A lot.

"A little." Leon helped him take out the plates

and mugs from the kiln. Some had been glazed. Some needed a second firing.

I might need a second firing.

Lord Jesus, I am so confused.

Why am I running away from the one I miss?

The one I love?

Leon walked back into the studio, walking by a partial version of his *Mother Memories* display. It was a three-foot-tall acrylic tank he had found in downtown Nassau. Incomplete, he hadn't poured resin into it and didn't have anything to glue on it.

In retrospect, he should have used industrial glue instead of homemade glue, but what was done, was done.

He picked up what Sophie would've called a "pile of something." He had tied kitchen pots and pans together. Fortunately, he had found old aluminum kitchenware. Otherwise, steel would have cost him quite a bit to ship from Nassau to Miami.

Putting down *The Kitchen Too*, Leon spotted Raymond in the small fenced yard behind the kiln. He was clucking to his chickens as he fed them grain. Beyond them a colorful coop stood like a bohemian cottage.

Leon made a mental note to incorporate those colors into his next oil pastel painting...

Of what?

Of whom?

He had only painted those oil pastels to show Sophie that he could do it. He had no one else to prove anything to.

Leon reached into his cargo shorts pocket to get his cell phone.

And remembered that he had sold it on eBay, together with most of his earthly possessions. All he had kept were his paint brushes, paint, oil pastels, art supply, and guitar.

As Leon watched the widowed Raymond shuffle back into the cooler indoors, he wondered what his own life would be like when he reached Raymond's age.

Would I live alone?

What would my perspective on life be like?

Well, he felt that he had at least forty years to think about that. Forty? Now how did he come up with that number? He had no idea.

Then again, didn't God own time?

What if I don't have all the time in the world like I want?

He realized the answer even before he finished asking himself the question.

Then I won't see Sophie again on this earth.

CHAPTER TWENTY-NINE

*L*eon had walked to Raymond's studio from his one-bedroom rental cottage so many times in two weeks that he could time his arrival down to the minute, come rain or shine.

However, on this Saturday morning, Leon had a hard time keeping his usual pace.

He had a headache from the lack of sleep last night due to the partying at the neighbor's house. No, he hadn't been invited, but his wooden cottage was so poorly insulated that he could hear every beat, every shout, every yell, everything.

Sleeping in would've taken care of it, except that Raymond's sister had knocked on his door before seven o'clock this morning with some bad news. Raymond had a stomach bug of some sort, and he had an art class at ten o'clock. Could Leon fill in for him?

And while he was at it, could he clean out Raymond's chicken coop and feed the chickens?

Four cups of coffee and a piece of stale bread later, Leon trekked over to the Raymond Fordham Art Studio, praying and hoping he knew what to do as a substitute art teacher for two hours. He was still waiting for Raymond to email him the lesson plan.

The art studio door unlocked easily, but before Leon could step in, he heard a voice.

A familiar voice.

He wasn't startled by it. In fact, he felt relieved. He knew the day would come and that they'd catch up to him.

He turned around.

"Hey, Jonah. Whassup?" Aidan Ming Wei was in a Hawaiian shirt, a pair of denim shorts, and hiking boots. He was wearing sunglasses with smudges on them. He held a coffee mug in his hand.

Leon waited.

"Considering you hadn't even bothered to stop using your credit card, and you flew out of the country on a valid passport, I'd say two things." Ming sipped his coffee. Took his time. "You probably don't have any malicious intent, and you want us to find you."

Leon didn't smile or reply.

"You want us to find you," Ming repeated. "And bring you home."

"Home?" Leon expelled a deep breath. "I don't have a home."

"Sure you do." Ming raised his sunglasses, which now perched on top of his mop of hair. "Savannah is your hometown. And Riverside Chapel is your family."

Leon grunted.

"You're not the only one who has lost a parent. I've lost both. I survived. You can too."

And Sophie had also lost her mom.

Long ago.

"How can there be so much suffering in this world?" Leon whispered under his breath.

"You know the answer to that," Ming said. "When sin entered into the world at Eden, it brought pain and death. That's why Jesus had to go to the cross. Paid for it all, He did. Praise the Lord. So now pack your bags, and let's go home."

Leon stood there. No words came to his mouth.

Yet in his mind, the reference verse from one of Pastor Flores's sermons spoke loudly and clearly to him.

These things I have spoken unto you, that in Me ye might have peace. In the world ye shall have tribulation: but be of good cheer; I have overcome the world.

Still...

"Okay then," Ming said. "Whenever you're ready to come home, we'll be there for you. Most of us, anyway."

Most of them?

Sophie too?

"Don't think your problem is so unique that you're the only one," Ming added.

"Are you here to lecture me?" Leon asked.

"Let me just say it as it is."

"That's how I prefer it, brother."

Ming nodded. "It's much easier for me to deal with people I don't know—fugitives and suchlike. I hunt them down all the time, as you know from my work. It's harder—hurts more—when I have to track down people I know."

"Okay."

"Everyone's worried about you..." Ming hesitated. "Sophie hasn't stopped crying. What you've done to that poor girl, I can't even begin..."

"I don't believe you," Leon said.

"Believe what?"

"Sophie is independent enough to go on without me."

"You left town—and country!—and you took her heart with you, dude!"

Leon leaned back at the painted door. "I...uh... we were just...dating."

"Maybe it has become more than that. Ever been in love?"

Leon shook his head. "No."

"Neither have I." Ming laughed. "Dated a few girls here and there, but I don't think I ever fell in love."

"So we don't know what it means."

"Right." Ming tilted his head. "All I know is that your church family is worried about you. We've been praying for you. Then we took up a collection to pay my PI firm to find you."

"So they paid for your plane tickets here?"

"Simon paid for my plane tickets."

Simon Kowalski.

Now Leon felt bad. Sophie must be in some world of hurt if her dad would pay out of pocket for plane tickets to track down a...

Runaway?

Leon wouldn't call himself a runaway.

But others might.

Ming slurped the last drop from his mug. "You got more coffee?"

"Depends."

"Depends on what?" Ming eyed him suspiciously.

"How desperate are you?"

"Oh, very. I haven't slept in two days—duty calls —and I need more caffeine."

"Good. Then you'll do anything." Leon smiled. "Let me show you the chicken coop."

CHAPTER THIRTY

*P*astor Dixon minced no words when his booming voice filled the sanctuary of the old Chapel by the Sea, calling his congregation to action.

"When God speaks, we listen, we follow!" Dixon pointed to the Sunday crowd.

Leon sat in the back, as per usual.

He had only agreed to come to church because Mom would've wanted him to keep doing that, wherever he went, no matter where he lived.

Besides, he had somehow ended up volunteering to fill in for Raymond this Monday to paint the rest of the church walls outside, and they had a planning meeting after church that he could not skip if he wanted to keep his word.

Keep my word?

Leon dug through his memories, trying to remember if he had ever given a word he hadn't kept, especially to Sophie.

Whoa. How did Sophie come to mind?

"Psalm 57:1. Listen." Pastor Dixon read his Bible on the lectern.

Leon followed along.

Be merciful to me, O God, be merciful to me!

For my soul trusts in You;

And in the shadow of Your wings I will make
my refuge,

Until these calamities have passed by.

Slowly, his eyes scanned the chapel underneath spinning fans.

Leon slid down his seat a little bit so that Dixon didn't see him.

This was the second Sunday he had been in church at Chapel by the Sea. He hadn't started attending any of the Sunday School classes yet, though Raymond had invited him to one, where his friend Byron Moss sometimes filled in for the teacher.

"Byron's about your age, so you two might have things to talk about," Raymond would say until Leon didn't want to hear any more.

Going to the church service was one thing, but

attending Sunday School would be a double conviction for him.

Right now, all he needed was more conviction,
right?

Yeah, after that visit from his friend Ming.

"In the shadow of the Lord's wings!" Pastor
Dixon let it sink. "That's where we find our refuge."

The sermon went on, and Leon thought the
pastor was doing a good job. That was, until he
came to the end of the service.

"Are you running away?" Pastor Dixon asked.

Am I running away?

"Are you looking for a place to hide?"

Am I hiding?

Leon shifted slightly on the wooden pew and
hoped no one noticed.

"Hide in the mighty shadow of His wings until
all these troubles pass," Pastor Dixon instructed.
"Let's pray."

Leon stood with the rest of the congregation to
pray.

He was quite relieved that this was a one-part
sermon. Next week, Pastor Dixon would be on to
some other convicting truth.

As Leon entered the hallway to get to his after-
church meeting, he felt someone walking next
to him.

"Some sermon, huh?"

Ming again.

"Whatcha doing here?" Leon asked. He wasn't irritated or anything that his friend from Savannah had been following him around.

And he wasn't surprised that Ming knew where he would be. He probably knew more than he let on, the private investigator that he was, with connections in the FBI and wherever else.

"It's Sunday, and it's church day. My flight is this afternoon," Ming explained. "Are you heading to lunch?"

"No, to a meeting," Leon said.

"What meeting?"

"Somehow I got recruited to help finish painting one of the outside walls of this chapel."

"Yeah?"

"Raymond's supposed to do it, but he's at home sick, and here I am with nothing better to do, you see."

Ming nodded. "So you're like driftwood."

Driftwood.

Sea glass.

Somehow Leon knew he had to finish that mixed-media piece he had been thinking about for the last couple of months.

He wanted to do his best to show...

Ah.

"Did I remind you of something? Someone?"

Ming asked. "You looked faraway for a moment there."

"I was thinking about an art piece I wanted to do. When you said *driftwood*, it reminded me that I need to finish it."

"That's good." Ming put two thumbs up. "We all need to finish what we started."

Finish what we started?

What have I started with Sophie?

CHAPTER THIRTY-ONE

*T*en weeks after Dad had broken his leg and could return to work at the gallery, Sophie began to settle on the notion that he was enjoying his time off too much to want to get back to work.

In the first weeks of his leg being in a cast, Dad had been antsy about getting back to his art gallery. Xian couldn't wait to get him out of the house.

Now...

After church on Sunday—less than twenty-four hours ago—Sophie had caught Dad and Xian whispering about going to somewhere warm for a few weeks.

A few weeks?

When would that be?

Who was going to run Simon's Gallery?

They hadn't said anything to Sophie about it.

She wasn't sure how long she could fill in for Dad. She had never been interested in the gallery. It was a business to Dad, yes, but there was nothing for her.

Sure, she had met Leon here, but...

Sophie glanced around, hoping nobody saw her feelings. She realized she was standing in the gallery.

How did I get here?

Wasn't I sitting down in Dad's office?

No, wait. She had been walking down the hallway...

Sophie sighed. She couldn't remember what she had been doing minutes before.

Or the hour before.

Or the day before.

Or the last three weeks.

This has to stop.

Lord Jesus, it's Leon, isn't it?

Sophie knew she had to let him go. Leon might not come back. Ming had reported to her and Heidi that Leon was in his time-out zone. Some emotional issues there.

Healing would take time, and Sophie was sure it had nothing to with her or anyone else at Riverside Chapel, really. Leon had to deal with something from his own past, and only God could help him.

Truly, God is all he needs.

Needless to say, Leon was on the church's prayer list, right on the very top.

Sophie's iPhone buzzed. A reminder about the next thing to do.

Life goes on.

Even if the heart can't.

Abilene Dupree was scheduled to meet her this afternoon, after Abilene's last class at SCAD. They were going to discuss ideas for the gallery's new art education wing next door. Now that the mold was gone, the renovation was underway.

As if on cue, Sophie heard the power tools.

She shook her head.

It was probably going to be like that for the next two months. She wondered what tourists would say about visiting a tranquil art gallery only to be met with the sounds of drills, hammers, saws.

As if on a timer, Sophie walked back to Dad's office. She had decluttered it and cleaned it up. But she didn't want to think how it would all go back to a mess after she returned the keys to Dad.

On the computer, she viewed the schedule for the rest of the year at Simon's Gallery.

It was early November now, and Dad would probably return to work after Thanksgiving.

She could then take December off and go visit her brother, Adam—if he was at home.

She felt that she needed to get out of town.

However, she couldn't do anything until Dad's cast was off. Xian couldn't run the gallery and take care of Dad at the same time. Adam was busy with work.

Sophie was left to pick up the slack.

She wondered what it would've been like had there been four or five kids in the family. Would everyone take turns to care for Dad?

Sometimes she worried a bit about Adam's job. It seemed dangerous to be a Deputy U.S. Marshal, but Adam always downplayed his risks. If something happened to Adam, Sophie would be the only one left to care for Dad and Xian.

I could never leave town.

CHAPTER THIRTY-TWO

*S*avannah looked the same way Leon had left it in October. Crossing the cobblestone between two buildings facing River Street, Leon reached the freshly painted expanded Simon's Gallery.

Now he saw what he had missed.

The glass door to the new space next door to the main gallery showed some sort of activity inside. Leon stepped closer, and saw people sitting at rows of tables, painting something. In front of them, away from the street, was apparently the art teacher.

It seemed that Simon had decided to add art education to his gallery. Leon hadn't thought the business needed any infusion of cash.

He entered the gallery through the old glass door.

Inside, everything looked the same as before.
Pieces of artwork and sculptures with clean lines.
Nothing overly imaginative.

Sophie must still be in charge.

As he walked to the only desk in the entire
gallery, he found Baxter staring at him. His face was
stoic, and Leon couldn't read anything. He decided
to stay calm.

"Hi, Baxter," Leon said quietly.

"You disappeared," Baxter said.

"I'm back."

"You can't just come and go. Breaks everybody's
heart."

Leon ignored him. "Is Simon in?"

"He's on a vacation in New Zealand. It's
summer there."

"The Southern Hemisphere."

"Uh-huh. As soon as his cast was off, he and
Xian flew out to Auckland. They're going to be
there until after Christmas."

Leaving Sophie alone?

Like I had?

"She's on the rooftop patio," Baxter said before
Leon could ask the question.

Not knowing what to expect, Leon made his
way up.

I *should go clean up the office and wait to go home.*

Sophie told herself that again, but she didn't move from the wicker love seat. The Savannah temperature around her was in the sixties, the sky was clear, and all she could hear was the sound of traffic three floors below.

Her iPhone showed four o'clock in the afternoon.

Sure, it was only Tuesday, but it had been a lazy one.

Baxter and Sheryl were capable of handling the operations downstairs.

Sophie felt that she could stay up here for a few more minutes. Dad wouldn't mind. In fact, he had gone on his hastily planned post-break-a-leg vacation.

He had emailed saying that he and Xian had arrived safely in Auckland and were taking a cruise around the islands of New Zealand.

And, oh yes, Adam had texted a week ago, asking when the Christmas family gathering was.

Sophie had to tell him—as nicely as she could—that this year, it would only be his little sister and him, if he still wanted to come to Savannah for Christmas.

Half their family would be in the Southern
Hemisphere catching some summer sun. The other
half should expect the weather to turn cold by
Christmas Eve.

"No snow?" Adam had replied to her text.

Sophie was glad her brother was coming
anyway, though she wasn't planning on being alone.
Heidi and Ming would be in town, and they had
invited Sophie to attend their annual Christmas
party for singles at Riverside Chapel.

As she reclined on the love seat, Sophie thought
that surely her fifteen-minute break was over.

Still, her eyelids were heavy. She felt exhausted.
Two months of running the gallery, and no vacation
for her. She had taken only one day off for
Thanksgiving Day. Then it was back to work the
next day because of Black Friday shoppers.

She could open her eyes to check the position of
the sun in the sky or to see what time her iPhone
said it was.

But she didn't.

No matter what, God has been good to us.

Dad's leg had healed.

Xian and Dad were on good terms with each
other.

Simon's Gallery had stable finances.

The art education wing was coming along
smoothly.

In fact, Abilene Dupree was such a good artist that Dad had asked her to paint some scenes from around town. She was going to get started on those watercolor pieces when the weather was warmer. Spring, probably.

"So much to be thankful for," Sophie said.

"Indeed."

Did someone say that, or was she hearing voices? Or maybe it had only been the sound of River Street traffic and tourists?

Slowly Sophie opened her eyes. Turned her head.

There, sitting on a wicker armchair across from the coffee table, was none other than the prodigal son himself.

Or Jonah, as Ming Wei had called him.

I let you go, and God brought you back.

Sophie held back her emotions, as if showing them would be a defensive sign.

Defensive? Of what?

I'm not the one who ran away to parts unknown.

Well, the Caribbean wasn't exactly parts unknown, but those islands were far away from Savannah.

Sophie sat up. Folded her arms across her chest. "Why are you here?"

Leon lowered his head. "To ask you to forgive me."

211

"I already did."

"You did?" Leon's eyes sparkled in the afternoon sun.

"The week you left. Took me a few days though."

"Wow. I don't deserve it."

"Do we deserve God's forgiveness for our sins?" Sophie asked.

"No."

"And yet He forgave us when we believed in Jesus Christ for the salvation of our souls."

Leon nodded. "Even as a Christian I still sinned by being selfish. I thought only of myself."

"While you were wandering around, Pastor Flores has been preaching on the new man versus the old. It's a struggle until we get to heaven."

"I'm so sorry." Leon took a deep breath.

He seemed to do that when he was nervous—or at least it was how Sophie remembered.

"I was in the Bahamas. Did Ming tell you?"

Sophie didn't nod or anything. She had asked Ming not to tell her where Leon had gone to, so he had simply said that Leon was in the Caribbean searching for driftwood, sea glass, and himself.

"I blamed my biological father for leaving us, and I blamed Mom for leaving me," Leon blurted.

"God never leaves us," Sophie finally said.

Leon nodded. "I went to a church in Nassau and got some grief counseling. I've already emailed Pastor Flores about it, and we're going to get together for some one-on-one."

"Here in town?"

"Here in town."

Does that mean he'll stay for a while?

"Someday I'd like to take you to the Bahamas," Leon said. "Show you the places I went. Take you to my friend's art studio. And visit Chapel by the Sea. Some good people there. I'd like to recommend that Pastor Flores organize a summer mission trip there. They have a summer day camp. They could always use volunteers."

Sophie wrinkled her eyebrows. "You're telling me all that because..."

Leon shrugged. "I don't know. I guess I wish that you were there with me."

"I couldn't have gone."

"Yeah, I know. Unlike me, who quits too easily."

Sophie wanted to say that she, too, had to learn the hard way regarding living by faith versus feelings, but it wasn't her place to correct him, when she herself still had more biblical principles to learn.

She decided to pray instead, hoping that God would show Leon what he needed to learn and when.

They sat in silence for a while, with Sophie trying not to look at Leon. He didn't look older, but he had a fresh haircut.

"I like your new haircut," Sophie finally said as the minutes passed.

"Thank you. My friend Raymond's niece owns a hair salon, and she gave me a discount."

"Raymond? Is he the same friend who also owns the art studio?"

"Yeah. He's a potter. He started the art studio decades ago with his wife, but she passed away." His voice tapered off as he said that.

"Death is always sad," Sophie said. "But in Christ we never die, remember? We go to heaven."

Leon nodded.

"Has it ever occurred to you that maybe God brought us both here for such a time as this?" Sophie asked. "Maybe we're meant to go through life..."

"Together." Leon finished her sentence.

"Sometimes it doesn't help to go back to where you came from. When God opens a new chapter, stop flipping the pages back to closed chapters. Words of wisdom from Dad."

"I'm working on that. Speaking of your dad, I hear he and Xian have gone to New Zealand."

"Yeah. First time we're not going to have Christmas together."

"So you're staying in town then?"

Sophie nodded. "Riverside has a Christmas Day party at Roger Patel's house. I don't know him very well since this is my first Christmas at our church."

"He probably joined when we weren't here." Leon seemed to be mulling over something. "I think this is my second or third Christmas at Riverside, but this is the first time I've heard of a Christmas Day event for singles."

"Heidi told me they started it last year. Mostly for singles who don't have families in town."

"Like us. So you're going?"

"My brother, Adam, is also joining us. He and Ming know each other from their connections at work, so when I mentioned him, Ming extended the invitation."

"So I'll finally meet your brother?"

Before Sophie could answer him, she grabbed her iPhone and shrieked. "Five o'clock! I can't believe I goofed off."

"I guess I'm rubbing off on you." Leon laughed.

"Not funny. I need to get back downstairs before Baxter thinks we're doing some hanky-panky up here."

Leon pointed to the sky. "God is our witness. We're sitting six feet away from each other."

Sophie slid her feet into her black pumps.

Leon kept up with her. "One question?"

"What?" She kept walking toward the door.

"Why did you forgive me so easily?"

Sophie stopped. Turned around. Stepped toward him.

She sighed. "Because I love you."

And then she wept into his shoulder.

CHAPTER THIRTY-THREE

*S*imon's Gallery opened the day after Christmas to accommodate shoppers. While there were no discounts for any of the paintings, sculptures, and art pieces, Sophie was glad to see a steady stream of people coming and going. Some carried shopping bags, but many seemed to be there to use up their time as they waited for others, who were perhaps shopping.

Sophie was at the front counter today, smiling and greeting customers. She had given Sheryl and Baxter several days off to go home to their families, who were out of town.

The art education classes were closed until the second week of January, so there wasn't much for Sophie to do. She knew she couldn't do it alone. Leon was only too glad to help.

Dad had agreed—via email from New Zealand —to hire Leon to help out. After the first of the year, he'd join Abilene in teaching art classes.

Still, the income wouldn't be enough for him to pay his rent. So Leon had gotten a job with Jerome Pendegrast's daughter, who owned Tamsyn Tours, which conducted walking tours and organized packaged cruises and vacations.

With the rest of his time, Leon kept working on his folk-art mixed-media pieces, hoping that some day he'd be recognized as the artist he was.

Still, there was no way Sophie was going to display his artwork in her gallery.

Hers?

Dad's.

So let's wait until Dad comes home, and he can decide what to do.

Sophie didn't think Leon was suffering. After all, the gallery in Miami had sold half of his *Home Life Too* exhibitions.

And word was spreading. Galleries in Atlanta and Nashville were talking about his art pieces.

Speaking of whom, Leon passed by her as he chatted with some non-buying tourists as they headed for the door.

When he came back, Sophie rolled her eyes.

"Did you drive them away?" she joked.

"To give us time alone." Leon waved at the otherwise empty gallery.

"We sold nothing today." Sophie glanced at the Dali-esque clock on the far wall. It was almost two in the afternoon.

"That's bad. Somehow you have to earn enough to pay for your Dad's four-week vacation."

"Ha. This is his gallery. His problem."

Truly, she had tried to help as much as she could. The art education wing had been her suggestion.

"Maybe if you display my *Home Life Too* pieces, you might change things up a bit," Leon said.

"We're not revisiting that."

"I know." Leon leaned against the counter. "I was stubborn too, until I learned to seek God's will, not my own will. I learned that from Pastor Flores last week in our grief counseling sessions."

"Are you calling me stubborn?"

Leon didn't answer. He was still on his art pieces. "I'm working on a new series."

"You don't need my approval."

"I want you to know."

"All right."

"It's called *Sea Glass.*"

Hearing it made Sophie reach into her purse underneath the counter to retrieve something that

Leon had given to her the day before at the Christmas party.

She had enjoyed the party, even though her brother received a call right in the middle of it, and had to leave to go back to work. Ming had given him a ride back to Dad's house to pick up his clothes and things, and then off they had gone to the airport.

Sophie hadn't asked Adam what it was all about, and Ming didn't say anything when he returned to the party two hours later.

Somewhere in the midst of all that, Leon had given Sophie a Christmas present.

"It's still pretty," Sophie said, holding the sea glass in her hand.

"Glad you still have it."

"It's less than twenty-four hours."

"I didn't have time to explain, but do you remember when you last saw it?" Leon asked.

Sophie could not remember.

"Remember that day you saw me toss a marigold into the ocean?"

"Yes."

"It's the same glass I picked up from the sand."

"Really?" Sophie lifted it against the ceiling light. "I can't tell. They all look the same to me."

"It's also the same piece I put on the magenta armchair on the rooftop the day I showed you the finished oil pastel painting."

"You did?" Sophie didn't recall.

"You didn't see it. So I kept it all this time. Took it with me to the Bahamas."

"And back again."

Leon nodded. "I have something else for you that I couldn't give you yesterday, because it was Christmas Day and I wanted to focus on Jesus."

"What is it?" Sophie was curious now.

"Open your palm."

Still sitting on the barstool behind the counter, Sophie opened one palm. "Please don't tell me it's a piece of driftwood."

"Close your eyes," Leon said softly. "Keep your eyes closed."

His voice drew nearer.

Sophie felt him swivel the barstool such that she faced away from the counter.

She felt something pressed onto her palm. It felt like paper.

"Open your eyes."

Sophie did and saw Leon standing in front of her. She looked down at the tiny folded envelope in her palm. It had sticky tape on it. "What is it? Can I open it now?"

"Go ahead."

Sophie peeled away the sticky tape, and a ring tumbled out of the envelope. She gasped.

Leon was on both knees in front of her, right

there behind the counter. He was holding a stack of four-by-six cards in his shaking hands.

"Will you please say yes?" He read off the card on top.

"To what?"

"Oh. Wrong card." He tried to pull another card out, when the entire stack of cards slipped out of his hands and scattered on the floor all around him.

Sophie put down the ring on the countertop and got off the barstool. "Did you number them?"

"Number them? Whatever for?" Leon laughed.

Before Sophie could kneel down to help him pick up the cards, Leon reached for her hands. "I know what I want to say. The words are sorted out in my heart."

Sophie's own heart skipped a beat.

Several beats.

"Do you remember when I said I had something to ask you later?" Leon began.

"Just before you skipped town," Sophie said softly.

"I left my heart in your hands."

"Eeek."

They broke out laughing.

"I think I've lost my train of thought," Leon said.

"Oh well." Sophie pulled her hands away.

"No, no. I'm kidding." Leon cleared his throat.

Sophie knew he was kidding. Two could play along. If she hadn't, she'd be weeping now.

Leon turned serious. "I fell in love with you that first day we chatted on the beach. I wanted so badly to love you all the way through, but I had hang-ups."

"Your dad."

Leon nodded. "But I'm not him. God doesn't clone people. We're all unique."

Sophie blinked a few times.

"Pastor Dixon and Pastor Flores both helped me to see that I must forgive my father."

Sophie wondered whether to add to that. She decided to do it. "And your mom?"

"Yes. And myself as well." Leon paused. His voice broke. "Once I forgave everyone, Jesus set me free."

John 8:36.

One of Sophie's memory verses.

Therefore if the Son makes you free, you shall be free indeed.

"Now that Jesus has set me free, I can love God. And I can love you."

Leon picked up the ring from the counter and then went back on his knees. "Sophie Joy Kowalski, the love of my life next only to Jesus, and who loves

Jesus too, will you marry me as soon as possible, so we can be together the rest of our lives?"

Sophie couldn't speak. She tried to process every word that Leon just said.

Tears pooled in her eyes.

"Is that a yes?" Leon asked, as though he had to be sure she knew what she was getting into.

"Yes," she barely whispered.

CHAPTER THIRTY-FOUR

"*N*ervous?" Sophie asked Leon as she drove Dad's SUV across the F.J. Torras Causeway that connected Brunswick to St. Simon's Island.

"Yeah. A little." Leon had been quiet for most of the drive. "But I have to come."

They were heading toward Neptune Park and the pier, where the outdoor Sea Islands Symphony Orchestra concert was to be held in a couple of hours. This was SISO's spring concert series.

It was outdoor. It was free.

And so here they were.

"I don't want to live my life reacting every time I hear his name or see him in the news." Leon stretched on the passenger seat.

"We prayed, so don't worry. I hope God will

make you less nervous once we get our picnic dinner set up."

In retrospect, Sophie wondered if Leon should have driven to their destination—to give him something to do rather than sit there and talk himself into depression or something.

He could have driven them to St. Simon's, and she could drive back to Savannah after the concert tonight.

However, Leon hadn't cared either way, so Sophie had chosen to drive in daylight.

She kept an eye on the traffic signs. Once on the island, F.J. Torras split into two. Either way would get them to the pier, but Demere Road would be a longer route.

She had been to St. Simon's Island before, with her parents on their weekend staycations. Dad had said that Seaside Chapel on the island was a sister church to Riverside Chapel. In fact, Seaside Chapel was still funding Riverside Chapel, until such time that the latter could generate enough tithing to be self-supportive.

As she stopped at multiple traffic lights through the island, Leon began to relax.

"I haven't seen him since I was two," he said.

When they reached the edge of the tiny island, Sophie realized that all the parking spots nearest the concert area had been taken. They ended up splitting up the work. While Sophie found a place to set up their camp chairs, Leon went to park the SUV.

~

*B*y the time Leon returned, having walked four blocks, Sophie had spread out their beach blanket on a patch of grass near the orchestral platform, putting two camp chairs on top of the blanket. In between the camp chairs was a rolling cooler, whose top they would use as their side table.

Leon frowned when he saw how close they were sitting to the orchestra. They practically faced the cello section. There were a couple of cellists there, with the rest of the platform empty, but they would be filling out soon.

Leon felt that when everyone was seated, he could almost reach out and take the principal cello player's bow away.

"Want something to drink, appetizer, or dinner?" Sophie asked, seemingly oblivious to Leon's predicament.

He did not want to sit this close to the front.

Doesn't she know?

Leon wanted to leave.

Sophie looked alarmed.

Suddenly, Leon realized what his purpose was.

Philippians 4:13 came to his mind. It was a memory verse that Pastor Flores had given him back in the winter when he was still undergoing grief counseling.

I can do all things through Christ who strengthens me.

Right now, he could sit down, stay with Sophie, watch the concert, let his father go, and then drive home.

Jesus Christ would enable him to do this.

Then he would have closure about his father.

Or he could leave and try again another day.

Sophie seemed to understand what he couldn't express to him when she suggested they move back. "We don't have to sit in front."

"But we don't have to move back."

"I think we should." Sophie was on her feet now, holding Leon's hand, and pulling him along.

They found a family of six crammed toward the back, where the sidewalk was between the grass and the water of St. Simon's Sound.

"We're sitting right in front of the cello section, and we don't want to be that close," Sophie told the mom and dad. "Would you like to switch places with us?"

"You're right in front?"

Sophie nodded. "Way-y-y over there."

"Oh yes. That's a great spot," the mom said. "Let's move."

Her children made a joyful noise, and the swap was easily done.

Leon felt better. Right behind them, next to some bushes, he could escape on foot on the sidewalk and run to the SUV.

If he needed to.

Lord Jesus, give me strength to stay put.

Someone came around to hand out the evening's program. "SISO also plays at weddings, did you know?"

"You do?" Sophie's eyes brightened.

"Yep. We do quite a lot of weddings all year around from Charleston to Jacksonville. Tonight we're giving away discount coupons to engaged couples who have a wedding coming up this year. Do you know anyone who is getting married soon?"

"We are!" Sophie flashed her tiny diamond engagement ring to the woman.

It was too late for Leon to tell Sophie not to draw attention to their upcoming nuptials.

Leon wished he had talked to Sophie about it on their drive here. He only wanted to see his father from afar. He didn't want to register for anything with SISO, sign up for anything, or do anything that would somehow let his father know he was there at all. He wanted to sit there until the concert was over and then leave as quietly as they had come.

"Oooh." The woman swiped her smart phone. "Let me get your names. When is your wedding date?"

"October," Leon said before Sophie could give the details. Theirs was a private wedding, and only family members and friends from Riverside Chapel were invited.

Family members?

How about my own father?

After the woman had gotten their names and left, Leon found Sophie reading the evening's program. There was still a bit of daylight left, but it was rapidly disappearing.

She was all over it, reading every page. "Did you know that Conductor Petrocelli is also the director of SISO? It must be a small orchestra."

"Don't care."

"Says here that he is pretty well known the world over, and has collaborated with orchestras in Budapest, Vienna, Moscow, Boston, you name it. Everywhere."

"Don't need to know."

Sophie seemed to be ignoring him. Her eyes were on the pages. "Did you know that his middle name is Leonardo?"

"Yeah."

"Bouvier Leonardo Petrocelli," Sophie said. "Interesting that your name is Leonardo Bouvier Watts. How come you don't have his last name?"

"It was Watts-Petrocelli for the first two years of my life. When my parents divorced, Mom changed my last name."

"Six syllables instead of ten."

"That too."

The concert started without Petrocelli, and Leon kept praying for calm.

Where was his father?

Leon had come from Savannah to see him— perhaps just this once—but he wasn't conducting tonight. Why?

After a boisterous piece, the conductor bowed, and Bouvier Petrocelli joined her on the platform.

He was tall. He had a bit of weight.

Is that how I'll be at his age?

But Leon couldn't tell the color of his father's hair. The sky was darkening, and the park had poor lighting.

Now Leon wished he had a closer look, but it was too late. They were no longer sitting in front.

"Please, let's hear it again for Avery Chung, our trumpet player," Petrocelli said. "This evening we're taking turns to conduct the different arrangements. If we have a brass emphasis, as we just did, then someone from the brass section will conduct. I will be enjoying the concert just as you are. Welcome to our summer series!"

As the orchestra played a variety of music—from classical compositions to movie soundtracks, and from children's nursery rhymes to more serious melodramatic movements—Leon began to wonder whether he should even confront his father at all.

Truly, all he wanted to do tonight was to see him from afar.

Now that he had, Leon hadn't felt threatened.

At all.

Thank You, Lord Jesus.

"I think I'm over it," Leon said to Sophie, who was munching on an after-dinner snack.

"Good. Stay calm, because he's coming this way, right behind you."

Slowly, Leon turned around.

Bouvier Petrocelli stood there in the cool of the evening, the nearby lamppost casting a grayish pall over his clothes. He cleared his throat, and introduced himself with a message from Leon's past.

"Your mother told me that if you ever come to see me, then it's time for us to talk."

CHAPTER THIRTY-FIVE

*F*ifteen minutes of intermission didn't seem enough time to make up for the twenty-seven fatherless years in Leon's life. He tried to focus on what his father was saying as they walked on the wooden pier to the edge of the covered benches.

Beyond the covered benches, the open sky with its twinkle of stars and cirrus clouds formed a canopy over St. Simon's Sound.

Around the two men, other people walked back and forth on the pier. Leon saw two guys sitting at the end of the pier, fishing in the evening. To the right of the pier, waters lapped on rocks and boulders that separated the water from a row of houses. To Leon's left, people strolled about on a small slice of sandy beach under the moonlight.

Mere feet above the sandy shoreline, Sophie was waiting for him on her camp chair, no doubt praying for them. Beyond Neptune Park, the island meandered toward the St. Simon's Island lighthouse, its lamp radiant and watching over the bay.

Leon felt God's peace in his heart.

Sophie must be praying even now.

"Alicia and I were never going to work out." Bouvier Petrocelli stood eye to eye with his son.

Leon could tell he had inherited his father's nose and chin.

He leaned against the weather-worn railing. Dipped his head.

"We should've let each other go long before you came long," Petrocelli added.

As if that would have made things better.

Leon thought of all the things Mom had endured all these years she had been a single mother. Those days they had lived on baked beans and white bread. Those days when water was a commodity.

There had even been a time—a few months— when Mom and Leon had stayed at a campsite because they had no other shelter, when Mom had been in between jobs.

How she had suffered!

And to think that after all those long years, she ended up with cancer.

Is there no relief for the poor, Lord?

"Your mom was so sick on the entire world tour," Petrocelli said. "There was really no relief. We had a hectic schedule for fourteen months, right in the middle of a very difficult pregnancy."

Leon had heard some of that story from Mom, but it was interesting to hear his father's take on it.

"Jet lag isn't something you impose on your pregnant wife, but my orchestra was the only way I made a living." Petrocelli took a deep breath. "In the end, she was too sick to go any further, and she ended up in a hospital in Bonn, while I continued our tour to Asia."

"You left her in Bonn?"

"My sister flew out there to stay with her."

Mom had left out that part.

All Leon knew was that Mom had been an only child also, and after her parents had passed away, she had been alone. Without more information, Leon had assumed that his father had left Mom alone when she had pregnancy complications.

"Trixie traveled with your mom back to Savannah, where she delivered you a month early."

"By then you were in Vienna, doing a collaboration on a new album." That much, Leon knew.

"Right. We were recording in one of the concert halls there. Very historic."

Am I missing something here?

"I couldn't come home."

There. His excuse.

"Couldn't?" Leon asked. "Or wouldn't?"

"I guess in retrospect I was married to my work, and my wife came in second."

A far second.

Petrocelli placed his elbows on the wood railing. "You do that to your life, and it's a surefire way to kill your marriage."

"So geography pulled you two apart."

"By the time you were two years old, Alicia and I hardly knew each other. She did her own thing, and I did mine. When we were together, there was nothing to talk about. The only thing I cared about then was the next album, the next collaboration, the next crossover music I could arrange for my orchestra."

Leon thought his father was about to ask him if he had heard his music, but if he did ask, Leon's answer would be no.

"Two days after my sixteenth album went platinum, Alicia filed for divorce."

"Wait a sec." Leon stiffened his shoulders. "What are you saying about Mom?"

"I willingly gave her half of my fortune. She had enough to take care of you without working for at least twenty years. You'd be in your thirties before you needed to find a job."

"How can that be true?" Leon's eyes widened. "Where's the money then? Mom and I were destitute."

"Beats me. Did she have a boyfriend? Maybe someone stole from her."

Leon shrugged. Mom hadn't said a word.

It made sense that she had lost the entire fortune somehow. Mom had spent most of her waking hours either trying to write a book or dealing with depression. She had male friends, but Leon hadn't felt any of them had been the right man for Mom.

"Anything I can help you with?" Petrocelli asked.

"Help me? What do you mean?"

"I'm not sure, but I felt like I had to ask."

Leon held his breath for a second while he gathered his pride. "I don't want any money from you. All I want is closure."

"Closure?"

In the distance, the music started again, plunging into beach music with orchestral accompaniment.

"Should we be heading back?" Leon asked.

"We're fine. I think my guest conductors can handle it. We'll be back there soon." Petrocelli seemed to wait for the other shoe to drop.

"Like I said, I want closure," Leon repeated. "I

didn't come here to talk to you, frankly. I came here to see you at work—from a distance—and to be assured that I have finally moved on."

"It doesn't matter if you don't see me again?"

"Not at all. In my formative years, you weren't there."

Petrocelli nodded. "For that, I'm sorry. I was full of myself. Please forgive me."

"You know, I have." Leon could hear peace in his own voice, reminding him that even when he had been fatherless, God in heaven had been his father.

"You have?"

"It took me twenty-seven years, but I forgave you," Leon repeated.

How could I hold a grudge when Jesus Christ did not hold one against me?

"Thank you," Petrocelli said.

"Thank God instead. God gave me strength to forgive you."

Petrocelli nodded.

Leon wondered if he was saved. Perhaps for such a time as this, Leon had been called to reconnect with his father. Something for him to think about.

Petrocelli produced a piano-shaped business card from his wallet and scribbled a number on the back of it.

"My personal cell number." He handed the card to Leon. "Maybe we can have lunch together. My wife would love to meet you. She knows about you."

Leon held the card in his fingers. He planned to keep it, but was anything going to come out of it?

If nothing else, it would go into his next *Home Life Then* mixed-media art collection.

CHAPTER THIRTY-SIX

The distant applause reached Leon's ears, reminding him that the concert had carried on without them. When the orchestra began playing another song, Leon was somewhat relieved by the interruption.

He had nothing else he wanted to say to his father. "I guess we'd better go back."

Petrocelli agreed.

But if Leon thought they were going to walk silently back to their own seats, he was mistaken.

Petrocelli had more to talk about. "We all cope in different ways. I hope you find your peace."

"I've already found my peace in Christ." Leon dared himself to ask the next question. "Do you know where your peace is?"

"It's in my work." It had come out of Petrocelli's

mouth so easily that Leon was sure he had believed his own words.

But it was the wrong answer.

At that split second, everything changed. Leon had been so full of his own emotions—again—that he had failed to see the need in his own father.

His father seemed to be saying that his peace—and perhaps salvation?—was in his career.

"As for me, Jesus Christ alone is the Prince of peace, the peacemaker, the peacekeeper," Leon said.

"That's your opinion. I'm not religious."

"It's not about opinion or religion. This is true for me and for millions of other people since the days of Adam and Noah." Leon hadn't expected the turn in the discussion, but he could only share what he knew in his heart. "When I was saved in Jesus Christ, all my sins were forgiven me, and God gave me peace in my heart."

Petrocelli grinned. "Yeah, if only it were that easy."

"It wasn't easy. Jesus paid for it with His life."

Petrocelli glanced at his wristwatch. "If you want, we can talk more later."

That took Leon by surprise also.

After not having been Leon's dad for most of his life, Petrocelli now wanted to meet again. "I suppose we could have lunch sometime, as you suggested earlier."

"I could drive up to Savannah," Petrocelli said. "My wife likes it there."

"Funny how our paths never crossed." Leon followed him through the covered porch, where colored lights lining railings on both sides allowed them to see where they were stepping.

"It's a bigger city than we think." Petrocelli nodded. "If your fiancée hadn't given your names to my assistant, I would not have known you were here tonight."

"How did you know that was me?"

"Your mother told me you go by her maiden last name. She also emailed me a photo of you playing a guitar—an old photo. You looked like you were in college or something. She wanted me to see that she did not discourage music in your life."

"When did she do that?" Leon asked. "She didn't mention any conversation with you."

"It was a while ago. I told her not to tell you about it. I didn't want you to hate me."

Hate was such a strong word.

"I'm sad, more than anything, that our family was not meant to be."

"We can't go back." Petrocelli turned solemn. "As for the future, am I invited to your wedding?"

Leon was surprised at how easy it was for his father to pivot from the past to the present to the future.

We can't go back.

"Sophie is handling all the invitations, so we'll check with her," Leon answered. "I'm sure it'll be fine, really. You're the father of the groom. What kind of an invitation should we send you?"

"Is that a yes?"

Leon didn't have the heart to tell him no. He nodded, wondering what sort of doors he had opened to an absentee father who was trying to be there now.

Before they reached Neptune Park, where the orchestra was going at it full blast—how else could Leon have described the sound?—Petrocelli turned to him.

"May I ask you a question?" the conductor asked.

"Sure." Well, Leon wasn't sure he wanted to hear the question—whatever it could be—but it had seemed that Bouvier Petrocelli was going to ask it anyhow.

"After your mother passed away, what did you do?"

Leon lowered his voice to hide his pain. "I took a trip around the world."

"That so? Sounds like how I would respond."

Respond?

"I would need to get away," Petrocelli explained.

"Find a place away from everything, everyone—to process what I'm feeling."

"Yeah."

"Then there's more of me in you than you give me credit for," Petrocelli said. "It was only in the last ten years that I bought a house and settled in one place. Before that, my wife and I—and our three kids—only rented. We moved from city to city."

"What made you decide on St. Simon's?" Leon asked. Around him, families with little children started to clean up and pack up. Others stayed on as the orchestra continued to play popular songs.

"SISO needed a director and a conductor. I needed a job. They gave me two."

"Funny how it's only one hour away from us —Mom and me—when she was alive." Leon frowned. "And we never talked."

"I talked to your mother when they gave her months to live."

Leon's jaw dropped.

"We only talked on the phone. We said good-bye." Petrocelli looked away. "But going back ten years ago, it was Alicia who emailed me about this job at SISO. Back then there was only a brass ensemble. Today we have a hundred-plus musicians."

"That's quite big for a regional orchestra."

"We're ambitious." Petrocelli seemed proud when he said it. "And we have generous sponsors."

"How does your wife feel about your ex-wife helping you out with your career?" Leon asked. Wasn't sure why he wanted to know, but there it was.

"At first she was unhappy that she hadn't thought about it herself." Petrocelli laughed. "Can you imagine that? I tell you what. When you marry, marry for life. Divorce is no fun. Remarrying can be a test of endurance. But we're all good now, Marisol and I, so nothing to worry about."

"To marry for life, you have to find the right person, right?" Leon did not expect an answer. "And only God knows who your perfect wife should be."

Petrocelli didn't say anything to that.

"Back to Mom, what did you talk to her about before she passed away?" Leon had to know. Wanted to know.

"That's between her and me, but I can tell you one thing." Petrocelli swallowed. "She told me to give you time. Not to contact you at all."

"Why?"

"She said if you want to have anything to do with me, you'll need to initiate the meeting, not me." Petrocelli patted Leon's shoulder. "And two and a half years later, here you are."

He seems happy to see me.

"Glad I survived the last heart attack so we could meet tonight." Leon's father laughed. "Otherwise, you'd be chatting with my tombstone."

Morbid humor aside, Leon hadn't expected to be on mending terms with his father this soon.

God had indeed worked on his behalf.

Now, after almost three decades, his father had returned in a near-but-distant sort of way that he'd have to sort out later.

Perhaps it was still not too late to begin a new chapter.

What Sophie had said to him on the rooftop the other day rang in his mind now.

When God opens a new chapter, stop flipping the pages back to closed chapters.

What kind of a new chapter was this going to be, with his father back in his life?

Well, wouldn't it be up to God's will?

CHAPTER THIRTY-SEVEN

*T*wo months and half a dozen phone calls from his father later, Leon Watts found himself back at St. Simon's Island for an overnight visit. He had planned to drive home to Savannah after dinner, but his stepmother had invited him and Sophie to church with her at Seaside Chapel.

The invitation had come in late May.

Since Seaside Chapel partly funded Leon's home church, he was curious about the mission-minded church. That had been his official reason for saying yes to Marisol Dalisay-Petrocelli.

The other reason Leon and Sophie had decided to stay another day was how Marisol had phrased the invitation. "Would you like to come to church with me on Sunday? The kids are on vacation."

She had implied she would be going to church alone.

After that phone call from the Petrocellis, Leon and Sophie had begun to pray for Leon's father's spiritual condition. They had continued to pray for him, even during their second trip this year, from Savannah to St. Simon's Island, for the Sea Islands Symphony Orchestra dinner at the conductor's house.

The Petrocellis lived by the marshes of the island, inland enough that Leon couldn't hear the ocean. Surrounded by green grass and live oaks, the sprawling ranch—with what looked like a new red roof—welcomed them to Leon's extended family.

Marisol held Leon's hands in hers as she greeted them at the front door, which was covered with scrollwork and Spanish flair.

"Sorry we sent your brothers and sister to Manila for the summer. They're trying to learn Tagalog. Otherwise I'm sure they would love to meet their big brother." Her smile was only second to her voice. She had a radio voice, Leon thought, something he could listen to all the time.

More than that, her words also warmed his heart.

Brothers and sister, not stepbrothers and stepsister.

The sound of shoes on the wood floor made

Leon look up. His father was saying something as he made his way toward them, but Leon had missed it.

"I'm glad you could come," Petrocelli said.

Yeah, I know it's weird for me to call him Petrocelli. He's my dad.

Leon believed that it would be even more weird for him to call his father by his first name, Bouvier. They were not fast friends yet, and they were certainly not on a first-name basis.

And I haven't called him Dad.

"Glad to be here," Sophie said to Leon's father. "Thank you for inviting us."

When Leon saw the spread of food in the formal dining room, he glanced at Sophie. Sophie turned to Marisol.

"Did you cook all these dishes?" Sophie asked.

Marisol laughed. "No, no. We have such an international group of musicians that each of them brought something native to their homeland—or something they picked up in their travels."

"Oh, we didn't bring anything," Sophie said.

"You're not expected to."

"I traveled quite a bit," Leon said. "I could have brought something for dinner. I learned to cook dim sum in Hong Kong.

"You did?" Marisol asked. "Then next time, cook us some dim sum."

Next time.

She wants to see us again.

Leon felt loved.

It was too warm and humid to eat outdoors this June evening, so the dinner guests scattered throughout the air-conditioned sunroom, great room, and even the foyer. Leon and Sophie wandered around with their plates, looking for a place to sit.

They ended up at the back of the house, in the sunroom where, before the sun went down, Leon thought he could see a river. He set down his paper plate on a side table, then stepped to the glass window to take a closer look.

"Is that a river?" he asked.

"It's the Hampton." His father's voice. "Feeds into the Altamaha River."

Like Leon was going to know where the Altamaha River was. He nodded anyway.

When he went to his seat, he noticed his father had seated himself on the other side of the side table. Leon thought someone else had been sitting in that seat.

Sophie came back with two bottles of mineral water. "Oh, would you like me to get you something to drink, Mr. Petrocelli?"

"Call me Bouvier," he said.

"Yes, sir. May I get you anything? Water?"

"I'm fine. Thank you." Petrocelli turned to

Leon. "I don't want *you* to call me Bouvier though. Someday, maybe you could..."

His voice seemed to have caught.

Leon waited, but the fifty-something-year-old man didn't finish his sentence.

Leon could guess what he was trying to say.

Someday, maybe you could...call me Dad?

It didn't take long for Leon to think that there might come a time when he could.

Yes, he could.

Someday.

~

*O*W*hen* Sophie had settled down on the other side of Leon, they bowed their heads together, and Leon thanked God for the food. Usually, Leon took his time praying, but this time he made it quick.

Sophie wondered if it was because he wasn't sure who else were Christians among the guests. Also, he might have felt uncomfortable praying in front of his father. She hoped that wasn't the case, but she made a mental note to ask Leon later regarding the thoughts that was going through his mind now.

On the other side of Sophie, a man with a scraggly beard extended his hand toward her.

"Ivan McMillan," he said. "Second string."

Before Sophie could respond, someone else in the sunroom laughed. She turned to see who it was.

A woman with wavy brown hair and what looked like an expensive striped blouse cupped her palm over her mouth. She was about two seats away.

"Sorry, Ivan," she said. "But second string?"

"Well, associate principal second violin sounds like a mouthful, don't you think?" Ivan replied.

"Or maybe just second violin?" The lady opened her mouth to say more, but her phone rang. "Sorry. I have to take this call."

She got up, put her plate on her seat and left the room with her phone.

Ivan turned back to Sophie. "I just met her tonight, actually. She's Ned Brooks's daughter, Brinley."

"I don't know who Ned Brooks is," Sophie said.

"One of the underwriters of SISO," Ivan said. "His father had started this orchestra some decades ago."

"Ah. I should've read up on the history of the organization before we got here."

"That's the gist of it." Ivan turned his attention to Leon. "And you must be Leon. Ivan McMillan. Nice to meet you."

Ivan glanced at Petrocelli. "Wow. You two look like an older and younger version of each other."

"Older?" Petrocelli guffawed. "Are you calling me old?"

"Ah..." Ivan looked alarmed.

"Just kidding," Petrocelli said.

"Whew. I couldn't tell," Ivan muttered.

Sophie heard it. She wondered what kind of a conductor and director Petrocelli was. That thought reminded her that she had never met Leon's mom either.

What kind of heritage does Leon have?

Was he more like his mom? Or dad? Or neither?

Sophie thanked God that Leon and his dad hadn't thrown each other overboard at the pier that Friday night back in April. There had been some friction—maybe a lot of it—from their past, and she had no idea what could have happened.

Sophie remembered praying the entire time that Leon and Petrocelli had taken their walk—on the plank?—while SISO had continued their free concert. She had prayed Leon would keep his feelings in check, put his faith in God, and that they would have a good conversation.

And now, two months later, Leon and his father would meet again.

Before the moment was lost, Sophie put down her dinner plate and reached for her purse on the floor.

"Let me take a photo of both of you," Sophie stood in front of Leon and his father. "Smile!"

Her iPhone camera flashed.

"Are my eyes closed?" Father and son said in unison.

CHAPTER THIRTY-EIGHT

*L*eon hadn't been entirely sure they should hold the wedding ceremony on the same beach where his mother had last walked on this earth.

Nonetheless, it was also the place where Leon had fallen in love with Sophie, a woman who had taken a long time to warm up to his folk art. Still, they had found common ground at their breakfast picnics and in oil pastels.

Most of all, they shared the same faith. And that had been the most important element for Leon.

So here, on this fine October Saturday, one year after they had fallen in love, it seemed fitting that they start their new life here, near their usual picnic spot.

Leon looked out to the Atlantic Ocean, wishing

Mom could see his choice of bride. He was sure that she would be happy and pleased. Most of all, she was with God now. And God was whom Leon needed to focus on.

Lord, I pray that You are pleased with Sophie and me.

As for Leon's father, the man had been busy warming up his ensemble of thirty orchestra members from the Sea Islands Symphony Orchestra. Leon could hear the various orchestra sections behind him, and his father's booming voice ordering them around, the tapping of his baton juxtaposed against the crashing sounds of the ocean waves.

Bouvier Petrocelli would've summoned more musicians from SISO if Leon hadn't put his foot down. Still, he had relented and let his father assign ten more string musicians to play during the reception.

Then again, it was all free.

Petrocelli's firstborn son was getting married, after all.

As for Sophie, she had been uncharacteristically giddy since the rehearsal dinner the night before and had continuously sided with Leon's father since the first day that their fathers had suggested live orchestral music.

Well, then again, Leon didn't care too much

about that. He could be flexible. As long as he and Sophie were married today, his father could bring the entire orchestra here if he wanted.

As Leon turned around, his white silk shirt and pants fluttered in the ten o'clock sunshine, reminding him to thank God for the clear weather and pleasant temperature this autumn morning.

Thank You, Lord.

They hadn't planned a long ceremony, to be sure, and they'd be indoors at the reception by noon, when the temperature was supposed to rise to the seventies. Right now it was in the comfortable midfifties.

He felt sad that the old house that Mom had dreamed of living in had been demolished, giving way to a coastal plantation-styled bed-and-breakfast, where the reception would be held.

But first the wedding ceremony itself had to be completed.

To say he was nervous would be to understate the gravity of this turning point in his life.

Leon had been antsy for an entire week, and the night before, he could barely sleep, waking up every other hour to be sure he hadn't misplaced the custom gold wedding rings he had designed himself, and which a sculptor friend had forged for him.

It had been quite an expensive set, but he had

planned only one pair for the rest of his life, so it was worth it.

Wandering around, collecting sand in his sandals, Leon wondered if they should've gotten married on the porch of the bed-and-breakfast or on the grass.

He shook off the sand in his sandals and then saw that sand had also collected on the cuffs of his pants.

"Messy, huh?"

Leon was glad to hear his best man's voice. "Not going too casual, even if it's a beach wedding."

"I hear you." Ming handed Leon his blazer. "At least we'll look smart, all dressed up...but with sand everywhere."

"Yeah, and I might just go barefoot." Leon put on his blue linen blazer. "What time is it?"

"Time to go line up." Ming pointed toward the house. "Diego is on his way."

Leon watched Pastor Flores amble toward them, dressed in a summer jacket. He had a Bible in one hand and a pair of flip-flops in the other hand.

As Pastor Flores came closer, Leon could her his own heartbeats thumping against his chest walls.

He wondered what was going through Sophie's mind this moment. She and her entourage of brides-maids from Riverside Chapel were still indoors.

As he and Ming took their places near Pastor

Flores, the orchestra began to play a soft medley of some of Sophie's and Leon's favorite hymns, which Leon's father had arranged himself, between the time they had reunited in May at that outdoor concert on St. Simon's Island and today.

Leon had no idea his father was such an accomplished composer and arranger.

He heard some of the hymns now and wondered if Sophie could hear them from her dressing room inside the bed-and-breakfast.

"Amazing Grace."

"In Christ Alone."

"Complete in Thee."

"His Robes for Mine."

"Run to Christ."

Leon held back a tear.

Oh, how far had he come. How far God had delivered him!

And how far he had to go, still.

Ming had been right. Leon had been a Jonah. However, he had returned home. Instead of running away, he had now returned to Christ.

And rested in Christ.

Praise the Lord!

CHAPTER THIRTY-NINE

*W*hen Pastor Flores pronounced them husband and wife, Leon lifted Sophie's veil, seconds before their pastor said, "You may kiss the bride."

Sophie thought she would be nervous and embarrassed to kiss in public. Thankfully, Leon made it short and sweet, though his eyes told her there would be more later.

Sophie hoped so, because Leon Watts was her husband now, and she would want them to be together always, as long as they lived. Their month-long separation in November had been too painful to recall.

Never again.

But now they had a reception to attend and a long road ahead of them before nightfall.

Leon held Sophie's hand as they waltzed down the sandy aisle to another medley of wedding music, mixed with ocean songs and the noisy but happy cheers of their guests.

Sophie's bridesmaid, Heidi Wei, and her brother, Ming, followed behind the newlyweds, keeping up the tempo.

As Sophie passed by the guests, she realized that almost all of them attended Riverside Chapel and were in the prayer group that had fervently prayed for Leon to seek and be in God's perfect will.

And God had answered their prayers.

She smiled to Dad and Xian, both of whom were beaming with joy.

Only Adam couldn't make it, called away to some undercover work and out of communication range for several more weeks. Sophie had wanted to reschedule the wedding around his work, but he said he would be on call year round, and even if he had cleared a Saturday for her, he might be unavailable at the last minute—as had happened over Christmas.

And as was happening today.

Sophie nodded to Leon's stepmother, Bouvier Petrocelli's second wife, with whom he had raised three children. All of a sudden, Leon had two sisters and a brother.

It had taken only twenty-seven years for poor Leon to have an instant family.

Then again, Riverside Chapel was his family, as everyone had told him.

And now Leon was starting a new small family with her.

I'll have to get used to calling myself Sophie Watts.

She had decided to dispense with a hyphenated last name. Too long.

Over the dunes and grass, the bed-and-breakfast was bedecked with wedding decorations all around the porch and across its large backyard, where outdoor tables and chairs waited for them.

Sophie tried to remember where the old path to the beach used to be, back when the old house stood there.

For some reason, she couldn't quite remember what the previous house looked like.

She wished she had taken a photograph of it, perhaps with Leon standing in front of it.

Let the past go.

She glanced at Leon, wondering if he knew what she was thinking.

He leaned toward her ear.

"Remember that verse? 'Therefore, if anyone is in Christ, he is a new creation; old things have passed away; behold, all things have become new.' Good reminder?" he whispered.

Sophie smiled. "Yes, good reminder from II Corinthians 5:17."

"I thank God for you." Leon gently squeezed her hand.

"I thank God for you too." Sophie sniffled.

"I'm famished. Wonder if we should eat everything or just nibble?"

As for Sophie, she couldn't think of food right now. All she could think of was their two-month-long honeymoon driving across the continent.

She felt partly excited to walk by faith in God and partly nervous that they didn't know exactly where they would end up.

Parked on the other side of the bed-and-breakfast was their home for the next two months, until the first of the year, when they had to either get back to work or find new jobs.

As a freelance technical writer, she could work anywhere there was Wi-Fi. As an artist, Leon also could work anywhere, as long as he had a place to put his mixed-media art pieces—preferably at art galleries.

Sophie had rented out her townhouse while they traveled. She had no car payment.

Leon didn't own a house. And hadn't bought a car since he returned to Savannah. He had rented a room close enough to Simon's Gallery for him to cycle to and from work. On weekends, Sophie picked him up for their trips to the grocery store.

Leon's art income was increasing day by day. Sophie was getting used to his folk art, which had shrunk to shipping sizes.

Since they didn't have kids now, they could do this.

When they had discussed with Dad and Leon's father about their plans to go on an RV honeymoon, both fathers had decided to split the cost and buy them a small used recreational vehicle.

Their co-ed wedding shower at both Riverside Chapel had been all about filling their RV with everything they needed for their journey. Some church members had made curtains, some had bought cookware and dinnerware, and some had given them gift cards from gas stations or for groceries, among everything else.

Their church had been generous, loving, and supportive.

They would need all of that, and most importantly, the blessing and mercy of God, as they embarked in their little RV on a new chapter of their lives: finding a place of their own to settle down.

Leon let go of her hand and put his arm around her shoulders as they reached their outdoor reception. To Sophie, it was like a giant picnic that they were sharing with fifty of their best friends.

After lunch, they would change into travel clothes, and leave their family and friends behind.

Sophie prayed for courage.

Courage to go with her husband—whoa, husband!—wherever God led them.

Leon wanted to drive west and keep going until they reached somewhere.

Sophie didn't have a problem with the apparent uncertain future, as long as they were in God's perfect will.

Still, she was curious.

Where would God lead them?

Where would they end up? In which state? Which city?

How about Arizona, where her brother lived? They were heading west, after all.

Regardless of where they settled down, one thing was certain: wherever God led them, it would be a wonderful place and time.

They had prayed about this, and Leon was certain God would lead them to an oasis.

Who knew—they might end up right back in Savannah. And her townhouse would be waiting for them.

Regardless, they would walk by faith.

Together.

And they would follow God.

Yes, together.

DEAR READER:

I hope you enjoyed reading *Ask You Later*, the starter novel in my Savannah Sweethearts series celebrating faith, hope, and love in Jesus Christ. The next book in the series is Pastor Diego Flores's story in *Know You More*. Follow along with Diego on his quest to stay in God's will for his life as he juggles pastoring a coastal city church and being in love with the girl of his dreams, Heidi Wei.

Know You More
JanThompson.com/know

JOIN MY BOOK NEWS MAILING LIST

Want to keep up with my writing schedule and get the latest book news from me? Sign up for my mailing list and read my newsletters for behind-the-scene information as well as to get free and discounted books.

Jan Thompson's Mailing List

JanThompson.com/newsletter

PLEASE LEAVE A REVIEW

Thank you for reading *Ask You Later*. If you'd like to leave a review, please follow the link below to see the retailers that carry this ebook.

Ask You Later
JanThompson.com/know

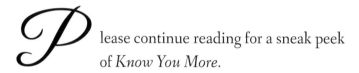

lease continue reading for a sneak peek of *Know You More*.

THE NEXT BOOK IS KNOW YOU MORE

SAVANNAH SWEETHEARTS BOOK 2

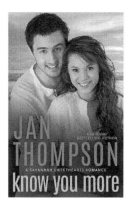

He loves her...
He loves her not...
She's waiting for him to decide.

A young pastor of a growing church in a thriving community, Diego Flores has to come to grips with God's will for his church and his personal life.

A Christian beach romance featuring life in a small church, *Know You More* is Book 2 in *USA Today* bestselling author Jan Thompson's Savannah Sweethearts series. This book begins the year after *Ask You Later* when Riverside Chapel moves its Sunday church services to a riverboat docked on the Savannah River.

DIEGO'S DISQUIET...

Diego Flores has been interested in his best friend's younger sister since their college days, but his calling to grow Riverside Chapel takes up most of his time.

When Heidi Wei becomes his strongest supporter in his church-planting ministry, how does Diego show his feelings for her without giving her the wrong idea?

Does she see him as potential husband material or just the pastor of their church?

HEIDI'S HURDLES...

Heidi suspects that Diego is sweet on her, but he seems to believe that his divine calling prevents him from acting on it. If it isn't meant to be, she's not going to push for it.

Yet every time they are together, something happens between them. Have they moved beyond the platonic relationship they have enjoyed all these years to something more personal?

When a crisis hits Heidi's family, Diego has to balance pastoring his congregation and ministering to Heidi without losing either one. Being in love while growing a new church is difficult for him to juggle. Which path is more important? Which one should he focus on?

Know You More (Savannah Sweethearts Book 2):
JanThompson.com/know

Savannah Sweethearts:
JanThompson.com/sweethearts

For book news, sign up for Jan's mailing list:
JanThompson.com/newsletter

KNOW YOU MORE CHAPTER 1
SNEAK PEEK

SAVANNAH SWEETHEARTS BOOK 2

"You can't be in grad school forever." Aidan Ming Wei flipped the salmon burger on his Weber grill. He left the cover open. On the other side of the grill, the chain-link fence stretched from bushes to sea oat dunes and then wrapped around the side yard of the old beach house.

"Why not?" Heidi couldn't believe her brother brought it up. Again. They'd been through this numerous times. Each time they'd ended up at an impasse.

"At some point in time, you'll need to get out there in the working world—the real world—and get a full-time job."

Heidi felt hurt at Ming's words. "Are you trying to get rid of me?"

"No—"

"Look, I offered to pay rent—"

"Not that." Ming reached for the platter in Heidi's hand. "I'm just wondering how many doctorates you need before any museum would hire you. You have one. Isn't that enough?"

Heidi said nothing. The aroma of salmon calmed her mien, and she was salivating at their dinner. Ming had always done that for her, cooking her favorite meals, taking her to her favorite places. She'd tried not to use the word *favorite* whenever she told him things, or he'd sacrifice for her.

There was no need, really.

She loved him regardless of what he did or didn't do for her. Ever since their parents died—

She sniffed.

Ming stiffened. "Let's talk about this later."

"No. Let's talk about this now and get it over with. What do you really want to say to me, Aidan Ming Wei?" She only called him by his full name when she was mad at him. That was getting increasingly rare since their parents had passed away. It had been seven years. "We've always been honest with each other. Out with it. I can handle it."

"After dinner."

"Now. You started it." Heidi followed her brother through the back porch, past his old hammock, and into the kitchen-cum-dining room.

"Okay." Ming set the platter on the table.

Heidi had set the table earlier. She sat down adjacent to him.

"Even the president of UGA doesn't have two PhDs," Ming said. "In history, no less."

"Meaning what?"

"Meaning there comes a point in time when school is over, you graduate, and you move on in life."

"I like being on campus."

"Then teach. You'll still be on campus."

"It's not about the money."

"Did I say it was?" Ming looked hurt. "I guess I'm thinking aloud, Heidi. We're in our twenties, but I'd hate to see us exactly as we are fifty years from now."

"But I love salmon. That can stay the same," Heidi joked. "Seriously, it's hard to have something different when..."

Heidi went silent and Ming didn't pry.

"I miss them so much," Heidi said.

"Me too." Ming reached for her. They held hands for a while. "But if you asked them, they wouldn't want to come back here. Heaven is perfect, and they're having a great time. We just have to trust God to take care of us down here until we see them again. All right?"

Heidi nodded. The tears flowed nonetheless.

"Heidi." Ming's voice seemed broken, defeated. "I'm sorry I brought any of it up. I ruined our dinner."

"No. You cooked me salmon. You made my day."

"You're so positive and I'm so negative."

"What are siblings for?" Heidi laughed. "You're right, you know. I need to be done with school."

"For the second time, Dr. Wei. Two PhDs. For what? Seems like a waste of time."

"Ha-ha. We'll talk later. Let's eat. Say grace."

Ming chuckled. "Diego was right."

"Diego? How did he get into this conversation?"

"He told me the other day—never mind."

"What did he say?"

"Uh, I said it first, so technically it's not his fault."

"Said what first?"

"You're bossy."

Heidi's eyes flared. "And he agreed?"

"For the record, he calls me bossy too." Before Heidi could reply to that, Ming bowed his head and began praying.

Heidi let it go.

When Ming finished, they ate in silence.

"I'm sorry," Heidi said when they cleared their dinner plates.

"For what?"

"For using up all my money to get these useless degrees."

Ming placed a warm hand on her shoulder. "Come to think of it, doctorates are not entirely useless. They're pretty good academic exercises."

"You were right, you know. What am I going to use them for?"

"You could always teach. Runs in the family, after all."

Yeah. Runs in the family.

Their parents had both been academic. Their research had taken them far and wide to study languages, cultures, and peoples. It was tragic that they had perished in that plane crash on their last short-term mission trip to the South Pacific. Their bodies had never been recovered.

Lost at sea and nothing left of them to bury.

Heidi watched her brother go for the apple pie they'd bought from the grocery store.

"Want some?" His piece was huge.

"No, thanks. I had some earlier this afternoon."

"That's why half of this is gone."

Heidi elbowed him on the way to the sink. She wrung out a damp dishcloth to wipe down their glass dinner table. They'd had that table for a couple of years. It seemed misplaced and mismatched, but neither she nor Ming cared. Much of their furniture was from their parents' old house in Jacksonville. The rest of the items were from donations, consignment sales, thrift shops, wherever they could find solid furniture they could use.

We.

But not really.

This house was not Heidi's. She had owned a townhouse once, but she had been so lonely there that she had sold it and used the money to pay for graduate school. Pretty soon she'd be running out of money if she didn't do something with her degrees.

Her brother was right.

You can't be in grad school forever.

～

*D*iego Flores stepped onto the small landing inside the front door. He wondered how Ming could live in such cramped quarters.

"The hospital rounds took longer than I'd expected." Diego looked around. He didn't see anyone else besides Ming. "Sorry I'm half an hour late to my own meeting."

"Late? We're never late for desserts." Ming took the container of cupcakes away from Diego. "You made these?"

"As requested. Where's everybody?"

"You know Nadine can't make it. Has to work. That girl doesn't sleep."

"Yeah. She texted me."

"Neither can Simon. He texted me. And Abilene is still in New Orleans visiting family." Ming stuffed a cupcake into his mouth. He could barely talk. It came out muffled. "Cam and Roger will be late."

Or something that sounded like that. Diego shook his head. "I call for a committee meeting, and half the people don't show up, and most of them didn't bother to let me know."

"Hey, we're a small church." Ming handed Diego a cupcake and a paper napkin. "What did you expect? A hundred people at this meeting? That's even more than the church membership."

"Don't remind me. Riverside Chapel is eighteen months old and all we have are thirty-some members." Diego plopped down onto a leather armchair just as his iPhone pinged. He checked it. Another church member needing prayer. No rest for the pastor.

"Tell me it's not Mrs. Untermeyer again," Ming said.

"You wish. Next time she calls, I'll forward her to your phone."

"Ha-ha." Ming sat down on a ratty old couch. His cupcake was down to crumbs.

Diego found it interesting that apparently Ming couldn't tell the difference in the ingredients. Diego hadn't put any sugar in the batter, only honey. Ming ate anything. Ever since their college days, whatever Diego didn't care to eat, he could always feed it to Ming.

Diego ate his cupcake slowly. Not bad, if he didn't say so himself.

He'd been nervous making the cupcakes, packing them, and driving them here. He was always nervous when he came over to Ming's house. He should ask God to calm him, but he felt that his prayers had been ineffective lately. So would God answer this special prayer he prayed every time he parked outside Ming's front door?

The other prayers seemed too easy compared to this.

For one, he had prayed for an increase in church membership. He had even given God the time frame and all. And yet, God had chosen to delay the growth. Obviously, God knew that if the church didn't show a trajectory of growth, he could lose funding from all those faith-promise mission funds at various churches he was affiliated with in the southern USA. They'd all want to see a return in their investments. His modest goal of fifty people by Christmas had been acceptable to his donors.

That was one thing.

This other thing...

Here. Tonight. Now.

He had to dislodge his heart from his throat every time he saw Heidi. Heidi with the wavy hair that swirled with the ocean winds. Heidi with the big brown eyes that saw through his heart and soul, and lips that asked to be—

He blinked.

Speaking of Heidi, where is she?

"Oh, she's in her room," Ming said.

Whoa. Had he spoken those words aloud? What else had he spoken aloud? "I was just wondering."

Ming grinned. "You've been wondering about my sister since UGA."

Diego didn't reply. Yes, it had been years since they were at the University of Georgia.

"Did someone say UGA?" It was Heidi's voice.

Neither Diego nor Ming said a word.

As Heidi came down the hallway, Diego could envision her in a wed—

"Hey." Heidi floated toward him but made an abrupt turn for a side table. "Ooh, cupcakes. Who made these?"

Ming pointed to Diego.

"Let's see." She took a bite. Closed her eyes. "Mmmm."

"Are you staying for the meeting tonight?" Diego's voice was raspy all of a sudden.

"Only for part of it. Have some research to do."
Heidi finished the cupcake. Took another one.

"I'm glad you like it." It was all Diego could say.

"Like it? Love it!" She wiped her lips. "Where's Cam?"

Why is she asking about Camden? Handsome, cute, eligible Camden?

Diego was surprised at his thoughts. He'd never pegged himself as being a jealous guy or anything like that.

"Cam will be late," Ming answered when nobody else said anything.

Diego settled on a couch across from Ming. "I guess we can get the meeting started. Latecomers can read the minutes later."

Heidi sat down next to Diego and leaned over to look at his iPad. "Ah, just as I'd suspected."

"Suspected?" Diego's palms began to sweat.

"Do you ever do anything without a checklist?" Heidi asked.

Diego had to think about that a bit. And then he thought some more. "No, I don't suppose so."

"What I thought."

"What do you mean?"

"Nothing." Heidi simply smiled.

"It saves time when you make a list."

"No need to defend yourself." Heidi leaned back where she sat.

Diego was surprised she wasn't going to sit somewhere else. There was plenty of room in the living room, considering there were only three people there at the moment. He didn't realize he was staring at her until Heidi nudged him.

"Pray so we can start the meeting, Diego."

"Yes, ma'am." She smelled fresh. Soap fresh, shower fresh. Diego cleared his throat. "I do have some exciting news, but it depends on how we look at it."

Know You More (Savannah Sweethearts Book 2)
JanThompson.com/know

Savannah Sweethearts:
JanThompson.com/sweethearts

For book news, sign up for Jan's mailing list:
JanThompson.com/newsletter

READ A FREE EBOOK IN THE SAME STORY WORLD

Set in Georgia, South Carolina, and Tennessee, this clean and wholesome Christian romance tells the story of art gallery archivist Sheryl Breckenridge and world-famous sculptor Winton Pace. Read this ebook for free!

Time for Me (A Vacation Sweethearts Prequel)

JanThompson.com/time-free

ACKNOWLEDGMENTS

Many thanks to my Georgia Press publishing team for keeping up with my writing schedule.

For this novel, I thank my outstanding copyeditor, Dori Harrell, and my patient proofreaders, Lenda Selph and Kim Kemery. Their eyes for details are from the Lord.

I am grateful to God for my husband and son for their support and encouragement. I also thank God for my parents and my three brothers for my happy and memorable childhood. I'll always remember my beloved mother and my late father for having instilled in me the love of reading and writing from a very early age. I miss my father here on earth, but I will see him again in heaven someday.

Most of all, I am eternally thankful to my Lord and Savior, Jesus Christ, who died on the cross to save me from my sins and rose again from the grave to give me eternal life. Without Him, I can write nothing (John 15:5).

Jan Thompson
John 3:16

BOOKS BY JAN THOMPSON

CONTEMPORARY CHRISTIAN CITY, COASTAL, AND BEACH ROMANCE

Seaside Chapel (7 Books)
JanThompson.com/seaside
Savannah Sweethearts (12 Books)
JanThompson.com/savannah
Vacation Sweethearts (8 Books)
JanThompson.com/vacation

CHRISTIAN ROMANTIC SUSPENSE AND NEAR-FUTURE TECHNOTHRILLERS

Protector Sweethearts (6 Books)

JanThompson.com/protector
Defender Sweethearts (6 Books)
JanThompson.com/defender
Binary Hackers (4 Books)
JanThompson.com/binary

Subscribe to Jan Thompson's mailing list:
JanThompson.com/newsletter

SEASIDE CHAPEL

Welcome to *USA Today* bestselling author Jan Thompson's Seaside Chapel Christian beach romance series. These novels are set on real-life St. Simon's Island, Georgia—a beach town where history is all around and the future is a moment away—and the neighboring fictitious Seaside Island, where the rich and famous live.

Savor the small-town atmosphere and the warm southern beaches of St. Simon's Island and the idyllic Golden Isles along the Atlantic Ocean. Enjoy the music of the orchestra and hymns of the church, and hang out with our Christian friends who attend Seaside Chapel, a little church by the sea known for its beach weddings and fair share of love and life.

As these Christians grow in their knowledge and understanding of God, they are tested in their spiritual maturity, their love lives, and their relationships with others. Share their heartaches and healing, and cheer them on as they celebrate faith, family, and friends.

- Book 0 (Prequel): *His Surprise Proposal*
- Book 1: *His Longing Heart*
- Book 2: *His Wake-Up Call*
- Book 3: *His Morning Kiss*
- Book 4: *His Quiet Serenade*
- Book 5: *His Waiting Love*
- Book 6: *His Beach Retreat*

For more information about Seaside Chapel:
JanThompson.com/seaside

SAVANNAH SWEETHEARTS

Welcome to the new south! From *USA Today* bestselling author Jan Thompson come these clean and wholesome, sweet and inspirational Christian romances set on the romantic beaches of Tybee Island and in the coastal town of Savannah, Georgia. Meet a group of multiracial and multi-ethnic churchgoing Christians who love the Lord, work hard in their careers, and seek God's will for their love lives. Against a backdrop of ocean, sand, and sun, these inspirational romances showcase aspects of the human need for God and for one another. Have some tea, settle in a comfortable reading chair, and enjoy these sweet celebrations of faith, hope, and love in Jesus Christ.

- Book 1: *Ask You Later* (Artist Romance)

- Book 2: *Know You More* (Multiracial Romance)
- Book 3: *Tell You Soon* (Asian-American Romance with Suspense)
- Book 4: *Draw You Near* (International Romance)
- Book 5: *Cherish You So* (Wheelchair Billionaire Romance)
- Book 6: *Walk You There* (Old-Meets-New Tour Guide Romance)
- Book 7: *Love You Always* (Romance with Suspense)
- Book 8: *Kiss You Now* (Multiracial Romance)
- Book 9: *Find You Again* (Multiracial Romance)
- Book 10: *Wish You Joy* (Christmas-Themed Romance)
- Book 11: *Call You Home* (Deaf Chef Romance)
- Book 12: *Let You Go* (Asian-American Romance with Suspense)

For more information about Savannah Sweethearts:
JanThompson.com/savannah

VACATION SWEETHEARTS

Travel with our friends from Savannah, Georgia, to the coast and to the mountains. Cheer them on as they celebrate the immeasurable grace and undeserved mercy of God through Jesus Christ.

The Vacation Sweethearts novels are a spin-off of Jan's Savannah Sweethearts series, and fans will recognize familiar faces from Riverside Chapel, a church in the coastal city of Savannah, Georgia. In fact, we might even visit the beach town of Tybee Island from time to time to visit old friends and beloved families...

- Book 0 (Prequel): *Time for Me*
- Book 1: *Smile for Me* (International Romance)

- Book 2: *Reach for Me* (Romance with Suspense)
- Book 3: *Wait for Me* (Romance with Suspense)
- Book 4: *Look for Me* (Romance with Suspense)
- Book 5: *Pray for Me* (International Romance)
- Book 6: *Care for Me* (Small Mountain Town Romance)
- Book 7: *Cheer for Me* (International Romance)

Read *Time for Me* (Prequel) for free:
JanThompson.com/time-free

For more information about Vacation Sweethearts:
JanThompson.com/vacation

PROTECTOR SWEETHEARTS

Private investigator Helen Hu and her associates specialize in searching for missing persons and hunting for lost treasures. Join them in their adventure suspense around the world in *USA Today* bestselling author Jan Thompson's Protector Sweethearts, a series of Christian Romantic Suspense with a side of mystery.

Protector Sweethearts is a spin-off of Savannah Sweethearts and Vacation Sweethearts.

- Book 1: *Once a Thief*
- Book 2: *Once a Hero*
- Book 3: *Once a Spy*
- Book 4: *Twice a Fighter*
- Book 5: *Twice a Convict*
- Book 6: *Twice a Soldier*

For more information about Protector Sweethearts:
JanThompson.com/protector

DEFENDER SWEETHEARTS

Defender Sweethearts is a sister series to the Protector Sweethearts Christian romantic suspense collection. While the heroes in Protector Sweethearts search for lost treasures and lost people, the Defender Sweethearts novels focus on protecting the helpless and hopeless. The main characters in Defender Sweethearts come from the supporting cast in Protector Sweethearts.

- Book 1: *Never a Traitor*
- Book 2: *Never a Hostage*
- Book 3: *Never a Fugitive*
- Book 4: *Always a Maverick*
- Book 5: *Always a Champion*
- Book 6: *Always a Guardian*

For more information about Defender Sweethearts:
JanThompson.com/defender

BINARY HACKERS

Like more suspense with your Christian romance? Like to read suspense thrillers? If you're looking for clean near-future romantic suspense without compromising the Christian faith, these books are for you.

From *USA Today* bestselling author Jan Thompson come these inspirational near-future cyberthrillers combining technothriller and romance, starting with Binary Hackers that feature computer specialists living at the edge of cyber-space, where they have to juggle being law-abiding truth-telling Christians while carrying out their assignments by any and all means possible.

The Binary Hackers series is set in the same story world as Jan's other books, and characters from the other series may make cameo appearances in this series and vice versa.

- Book 1: *Zero Sum*
- Book 2: *Zero Day*
- Book 3: *Zero Base*
- Book 4: *Zero Trust*

For more information about Binary Hackers:
JanThompson.com/binary

ABOUT JAN THOMPSON

USA Today bestselling author Jan Thompson writes clean and wholesome contemporary Christian romance with elements of women's fiction, Christian romantic suspense with an air of mystery, and inspirational international thrillers with threads of sweet Christian romance. Jan's books are for readers who love inspiring stories of faith, hope, and love in Jesus Christ.

Raised on a tropical island in the eastern hemisphere, Jan now lives and writes in the western hemisphere. Her international background gives her a unique multicultural and multiracial perspective to her novels and books. The island has never left her, and she reminisces about beach life in her beach romance novels.

When Jan is not busy writing small-town stories, she writes big-city romantic suspense and international technothrillers, a nod to her previous career in computer science. She weaves technology with human interests, reflecting the current and future digital world. And romance. There's always romance.

Beyond the printed page, Jan is a wife, mother, family scribe, avid reader, occasional artist, erstwhile pianist, and chief of staff to the family cat.

Find out more about Jan Thompson:
JanThompson.com

Subscribe to Jan's book news mailing list:
JanThompson.com/newsletter

For God so loved the world
that He gave His only begotten Son,
that whoever believes in Him
should not perish
but have everlasting life.
—John 3:16

Made in the USA
Middletown, DE
05 July 2024

56926896R00189